Praise for

DANNY
THE
AMBULANCE

"Have you ever seen Danny Welle's adaptation of
Danny Kafka's *The Trial*? Danny Joseph's Danny
The Ambulance is there, in the Jury Room dive
bar, and we might be drunk but it seems like nothing is what it seems. Danny Joseph invites us into
a verisimilar reality like Danny Egger's *The Light-
house* or Danny Bergman's *Persona*, but he does it
in a way that is whip crack smart and sardonic
and decidedly modern. When all of art and pop
culture and identity are simply echoes of each
other across an uncanny valley, this author cries
out, reminding us, Oh Danny boys, the archetypes, the archetypes are calling!"
— Danny Bender, author of *Dangerous Women* and
Kinderkrankenhaus

"Jared Joseph's glittering debut makes me feel
like God just thumped me over the head and
gave me a lollipop. Sebaldian in the structure of
its traversal and Delillo-esque in the abjection of
its humor, this novel transports me to the spaces
between dreams, where identity becomes oblique
as we move from the particular to the universal.
Joseph invites me to unearth the insidious Danny
that endures inside all of us."

— Danny Sijun Lou, writer and fiction editor at
Fence

"Funny and touching and weird as sex, Danny the Ambulance carries us and our wounds into a renamed world of Danocratic possibility, a biblically dark bar where creation is as accessible as repetition is inescapable. This book might eat you alive, but that way unity. In Jared Joseph's poetry and prose, the word is always God."
— Danny Dahlin, author of *Natch*

"A remarkably entertaining fusion of art, humor and morality. Joseph is half-poet, half-man."
— Danny Tottenham, author of *Fresh Failure*

"I am tempted to say Calvino, Gogol, Ionesco, Saramago. I am tempted to say absurd, hallucinogenic, uncanny, labyrinthine. DANNY THE AMBULANCE is the weirdest new novel I have read in years. It not only recounts, describes, entertains, and narrates, but also thinks—it is a rare thinking and thought-provoking novel. And what does it think about? Everything. The latent and the manifest, the contemporary and the historical, the unreal and the all-too-real."
— Danny Bassett, author of *Gad's Book*

Danny
the Ambulance

Jared
Joseph

The Shortish Project | San Francisco
theshortishproject.com

Joseph, Jared
Danny the Ambulance / Jared Joseph
ISBN 9798987839874

Cover art by Julie Novakofski

An excerpt of this work has appeared in *Heavy
Feather Review*.

The Shortish Project is dedicated to expanding
access to short novels, an open-door program
welcoming all styles and genres. For more
information and titles, visit theshortishproject.com.

Available in print and ebook editions
September 2023

the
**short
ish**
project

Danny
the Ambulance

Table of Contents

A record of public events or of a series of public transactions, noted down as they occur day by day or at successive dates, without historical discussion.

— Daniel Defoe, *A Journal of the Plague Year*

Part I
The part without quotation marks

The bar is called the Jury Room, it's across from a courthouse, between the two is the main thoroughfare Mission Street and the main river the San Lorenzo, brown, dirty, rushing in the rain, not a bird on its surface, hard to imagine a fish underneath it. The bar isn't small or large, it's between a taqueria and a Dollar Tree, there are 3 parking spots for the Jury Room, I've walked here so it doesn't concern me directly, but seems to bode positively, too, I think I'm the only person in the world who walks to bars and, if that's so, there should be 3 other customers here, tops. On Mindhunter there's an episode about the Jury Room, it's in the 60s and this is the 2020s, so that's some distance in time, but the lights are bright and the bar is bustling with businessmen, and lawyers from the courthouse, and Ted Bundy is a regular patron, and it's a fictional show but it's historical, too, and I like that in a show. I like when it's fictional and it's historical. It reminds me of my dreams, it makes my dreams feel less boring. I think the name Jury Room is strange for a bar because a bar to me feels like the last place for judgment, there is no jury of your peers, though sometimes it feels like the beers sentence you, but that's why the bartender clears the bar, so you lose count of what you've done. Even a serial killer can get a drink and the bartender won't bat an eye, the regulars won't, the irregulars won't. I moved to Santa Cruz for the same reason, because it seems like a giant bar, the anonymity of it, if anyone talks to you you can grunt, you can respond in human language, you can carry on with silence, and if ignoring the interlocutor gets the interlocutor going, the bartender will stop the interlocutor eventually, or even give you a free drink. I used to bring books to bars but it gets people to talk to you more often, and it gets me into fights more often, What are you reading, someone asks, Nothing now, says I, a fight ensues. So I stopped bringing books because they're too dangerous. I read the TV. I like surfing, the waves don't know your name, I'm gonna like Santa Cruz, like living in a slow wave, on a slow wave, under a slow wave, I don't know which.

The Jury Room is a wraparound bar, the light in the sky's just gone out, the lighting of the bar is very poor, in the middle of the bar above the bartender is one big fluorescent bulb, the further you get from it the dimmer you and everything else are. There's a pool table in the center of the room with a blimp-shaped Budweiser lamp above it, as of now unlit, there are three booths beyond the pool table, the wraparound side of the bar is directly under a TV, another source of light in the bar, if you sit there you can't watch the TV, people can watch you and the TV at once. I'm anxious about watching the TV, I don't want to watch the TV, and I don't want the person sitting under the TV to think I'm watching him, I sit under the TV. I thought I liked watching TV. I don't want to watch TV today. I'm the TV.

There's a man playing pool alone, there's no 8 ball, it's like there's no consequences.

He's humming to himself in a black leather jacket, Rolling Stones t-shirt, black jeans, Mick Jagger haircut with black hair, he's gonna die of brain cancer in 5 years. He gets tired of beating himself in pool and of winning in pool, asks for another shot and Corona back. He has a southern California accent as he says to me

This song, Human Fly, you know this song? Craziest thing, the Cramps did it, but originally by the Tune Rockers, they wrote a song called Green Mosquito. But that song didn't have lyrics, but the Cramps liked the tune, so they kept it and wrote lyrics to it. "I'm a human fly, and I don't know why, I go buzz buzz buzz, and it's just because" but it's a buzz sound on the "because," and then it ends "I'm an unzipped fly," it's like the Metamorphosis by Kafka but the opposite direction, the bug becomes a man, or the bug becomes the contents of a man's unzipped fly, which is his dick, which is metonymy for a man. I got this shirt at Urban Outfitters today and I think it's a little tight, and I picked up this silk scarf, too, at Moon Zooom, you know it? The cashier at Urban is really cute, she was playing the Cramps today, I think she thinks I'm gay, but I just want to impress her, you know, with this scarf, I think she'd like it. You want a shot?

I say yes I want a shot but he doesn't offer to buy me one. I think some people think they're generous. It's like he wants to know if I'm interested in drinking more, out of curiosity. I ask him if anyone else ever plays pool with him.

No man I'm not competitive. It's just kind of a meditative thing, I come to the Jury early to exercise my hand-eye coordination a little bit, my only enemy is myself, but everyone else is my friend. Someone comes in and challenges me to pool and I just hand them the pool cue and say Rock on, brother. Then I sit on my stool and think about my music. It's crazy how expensive CDs are today, and no one even buys them. I know there's a high supply but there's no demand, so why are they still so expensive? Mostly my record collection is my pride and joy, it's only growing, but it's still more expensive. But there was a yard sale down Lincoln by the Nickelodeon and I picked up a Legendary Pink Dots album that's out of press, thing's worth tens of dollars, I got it for 75 cents. It was a good day, haha. I'm pushing 50, so it's not often I have a day worth remembering.

I ask him what time it starts filling up in here.

Usually after I've had a few tall ones, he says, but it's real quiet today. Hey, you're alright. You're a good listener. It's rad talking to you. What's your name? My name's Danny.

Danny and I talk for a while until I get viciously bored. Then it's just Danny talking but, I realize, it's mostly been Danny talking anyway. He's been listing off the scarves he's bought this past week, price, color, material, and the girl at Urban Outfitters who helps him pick them out. He calls her "the girl," she helps him every time he goes in, which is often, it seems, and I don't know that he knows her name. I wonder why he doesn't know her name, or if he doesn't tell me her name so that I won't go in asking her, whenever he says "the girl" he casts a furtive glance at me, and then a furtive glance around at everyone else, which is no one. I wonder whether the bartender is listening, what she thinks of this, if she ever goes to Urban Outfitters, if she knows the name of the girl.

A boy walks in who looks like a boy, like he's underage, but the Jury Room doesn't seem like the kind of bar to judge that. There's an ID scanner at the far corner of the bar next to the bartender's phone plugged into the aux chord, but I can see the phone is new and shiny, and the scanner is dusty and with liquor stains on it, even the liquor stains are dusty, there's dust of different hues, or shades, but not of colors. The boy is in a big black tee shirt and baggy blue jeans and he has the eyes of a doe facing the barrels of many shotguns, his eyes are darting around like he has the name of a girl that works in retail that is his prized knowledge that prying eyes are trying to discern, to key open. He goes to the bar and asks if he can possibly have a Modelo. Of course he can possibly have a Modelo, the bartender says, mirthless. I think about all the martyrs in the world. St. Andy flayed alive. St. Sebastian gone clubbing. St. Stephen got stoned. St. Joan Baez. I don't know how old all these people were, but I feel like being young increases your chances of martyrdom exponentially. Do people grow up and think, when I grow up, I don't want to grow up. When I grow up, I want to die canonically early. Danny has gotten up to go to the jukebox, a dim little jukebox I hadn't noticed at the bar's other end that lights up and begins playing when he puts a quarter in it, because there's an agreement between the iphone and the aux chord and the jukebox, if the jukebox gets paid the iphone's played no longer. This technology interests me more than drones, more than vaccines, more than gene crispers, the play of submission and suppression between technologies, when one technology says Sit to another technology, and it sits and wags its tail. The maybe underage youth sits next to me.

Have you ever heard of the Madonna complex? he asks me. This is not his first bar of the day, I think, or at least drink.

You mean Mary Magdalene vs. Mary Christ? I say.

I don't know all about that, he says, I mean Freud. You ever read Freud?

I nod my head.

Freud says we all, I mean men, men are split in half and there's the type of girl they're in love with but they don't want to fuck them because that would be sinful. And then there's the type of girl they want to fuck but they're not in love with them, and then when they fuck them, they don't want anything to do with them, they want to get away. And I read this the other day and I was like, Wow. I have that real bad, I thought, he says. And then I told my friend about it and he got quiet. And then I said to him What's up, and he just said Wow, too. And he said That makes a lot of sense. You get that? the kid says to me.

And I say I don't know, it sounds like the Mary Magdalene and Mary Christ thing.

Who's Mary Magdalene? he says

And I say she's the biblical figure who's a whore, she's called a whore, but she becomes Jesus' first follower.

Oh, you mean the Virgin of, he says, the Virgin of, I forget what she's the virgin of.

I'm talking about the whore, I say. But you mean the Virgin of Guadalupe.

Yeah! When you said Mary Christ I didn't know what you were talking about. But growing up we called her the Virgin of Guadalupe. I'm Mexican, but I look really white. I moved to a new high school and everyone thought I was white, but I wasn't white, and no one else was white. I wanna learn to box. So I can puff up my chest like this, he says, and puffs up his chest.

But you're already puffing up your chest, I say. You don't know how to box but you're puffing up your chest, you don't need to train to do that.

No but you know what I mean. The way I get out of fights is making jokes. But I always get into fights, or almost get into fights, because I'm always fucking with people. I don't know why I fuck with people. There was a guy walking down the halls, and I stuck a stick of gum down his shirt. I don't know why I did it, it was unwrapped, I thought it was funny. And then he gets in my face and says You wanna get faded? And I say No, I just smoked some weed. And he says Haha, me too, and then turns and walks away. Because, you know, getting faded. So I get out of the fight because I make him laugh. He forgets about the gum even. But I don't know why I do these things in the first place, he says.

I don't know why either, I say. Probably Freud doesn't know either. The virgin of Guadalupe, that Mary, she didn't get fucked, she just gave birth to god when god didn't fuck her. So we idolize her and that kind of fuckless love. And then there's Mary Magdalene, whose love is carnal and earthly, but she renounces fucking when she follows Jesus, she makes Jesus a religious figure with authority by giving up sex work. So if you're stuck in the Madonna Complex, I guess, you're fucked either way, or you're not getting fucked, because fucking is bad in either category. But I don't really experience this because I'm Jewish, I say.

Are you practicing? he says.

No I'm not practicing and I don't believe in anything, I say.

Are you an atheist? he says.

And I say that I don't know, I don't believe in god, but I don't have a measuring device that tells me there's no god, so I don't know. But I don't think I can believe in one, it doesn't make sense to me.

Man, he says, I feel the same thing. I want to say I'm an atheist, but I don't know what I believe, you know. Like I don't know that I don't believe. So am I an atheist?

And I say that atheism and agnosticism are kind of the same thing, in word roots. a- means without, and theism is the belief in a god, so you're without belief in a god. And then a- again, without, and then gnosis, or knowledge, so you're without knowledge. And god is in charge of knowledge and knowing, even though we ate the fruit in the garden or whatever, I say. But I think they're similar enough, and you don't have to be either one, because they're not religions, they don't have followers themselves.

How do you know this shit, the kid says.

I don't know, I say. Wikipedia is free.

Hey man, this is really helpful for me, he says, it's giving me perspective. My name's Danny.

The Jury Room feels like a long thin unendurable shack and the rain pouring down overtop has the cadence and impact of tiny hammers falling on it. With climate change heralding the introduction of continual atmospheric rivers in the western United States the electrician is king, so that is what I am, King Electric, a business name that makes me shudder but that I know will do well in Santa Cruz because of its quirkiness mixed with its vaguely libertarian undertones. Surf communities are famous for this paradox or contradictoriness or whatever someone should call this knotty gnarly thing that simply doesn't make sense until you think of the most elementary psychology, the behavioral atmosphere of chill and mellow outlook, paired with the militant and despotic programme to enforce chill and mellow behaviors; this is our ocean and this is our surf and we will not die to protect it, but we will kill. Or if you think of surf and turf, surf is pacific flow and turf is querulous propriety. We love our beautiful land on which we read mandalas and consider the phases of the moon that tame and wild our oceans, and no government will ever interfere with the spirituality of our earthly existence. That's why there's smoking bars in Santa Cruz. But paired with this do-it-yourself laissez-faire entrepreneurial spirit of the beach town, this individual streak that pretends towards community, is a lack of infrastructure to guard the town against climactic disruption and catastrophism that a government agency is designed to step in to handle; basically, just a forecast of rain can cause a power outage in twenty neighborhoods. I couldn't have predicted this boon to business, but I can bask in and rule over it. At least this is what I say to Danny, much of this is what I say to Danny, and it's full of unearned judgments I haven't even made about a place I've only just moved to and barely observed. I have a habit of lying, at least this is what a lot of people who know me well would say about me, but those who know me really really well would say, well, he just likes talking. He likes creating something out of nothing, which is what talking is. No one would say that last part. No one knows me that well. I'm not saying I'm unknowable, that that's particular to me, I'm just saying no one knows me that well, I'm convinced of it. I'm not saying no one can know me. I'm just saying I don't know. I don't know.

While talking to Danny I hadn't noticed the woman who had come in and is now reading a book a couple stools away at the bar. Danny's gone now and I'm two drinks in and I don't know where he'd started but I know where he isn't, which is here, and it's cleared the optical way to see this woman reading at the bar. When you've been going to bars as long as I have you learn that there aren't really goodbyes and there are barely hellos, it's all in medias res, you're just in the conversation, and then there's a certain point that you're not. You don't even always notice that point. I used to read at bars until I got frustrated with being interrupted reading at bars, and it was always the same thing: What are you reading, someone would say, and I'd say Well nothing now, and that would either cause a fight or, worse, the interlocutor wouldn't notice the tone and would continue asking about it, and then they would tell me everything they've ever read in their life, which almost invariably wasn't much, and then they would ask me how I can read in a bar, and why, and then eventually they were just talking about themselves. I know I've already said this. I know I've already said this but what I said before was sort of different. I know I'm drunk already and I know I'm drunk already because I'm talking too much and it isn't consistent, like how I keep ordering the same drink but eventually the same drink tastes different, bourbon tastes like diesel until the fourth time it tastes like caramel corn. The thing I like about bars is I don't actually have to talk about myself, any question is a pretense to get the questioner going about what they actually want to talk about, which is themselves, and then they go, and I almost never have to talk again, I just listen. But I don't know that I like listening. I know that I hate talking. But do I hate being drunk I don't know. I don't know.

The woman is reading the book but more than reading the book is crying over the book. It's not soft tears but sobs and shudders and sometimes she lifts the open book and closes it over her face, like it's trying to eat her. But books don't have teeth or gums. But still it's a hardcover and I feel like repeated smacks are going to have a cumulative effect, like how a glass cup microfractures every time you knock it against a surface, even gently, until it chips. The point of actual cracking is not a sudden event but one that's been taking place almost stratally, layers and layers of invisible damage. Maybe I'm just talking about my personality now. I'm not talking at all actually. This is why I just listen, but I wonder if listening to drunks is the same as a glass being softly battered all of the time.

Are you okay, I say to the woman whose glasses are fogged with emotional condensation. Is the book that bad, I say.

She turns her head slowly toward me, a rotation of the face while she cradles the back of the head with her palm so her elbow is splayed now on the bar, face at degree 0 and elbow at degree 180. Directly above her hangs from a thin wire a plaster-cast baby with blood on it. The blood is not on its mouth, as you would expect, but blotching both its elbows. I think about Rorschach images, this is a red blot, what does the left elbow blood blot resemble to me? It resembles a baby hanging from a wire from the ceiling of a dark bar with blood on its elbows. Why did I not notice this baby before, I wonder. It's a noticeable baby. Are there other babies I'm not noticing, I wonder. What do you think of the Iliad, she says to me.

Wut, I say.

What do you think of the Iliad, she says to me.

By Homer? I say.

Yes, she says.

I don't really have thoughts about the Iliad, I say. What do you think of the Iliad?

When I think of the Iliad, the woman says, I think of its relation to the Odyssey. And then I think of the relation of the movie Alien to its sequel, Aliens. They're completely disparate genres because their scales of action are so different, and their concerns. Alien is a psychological horror thriller that happens to be set in space. But it's all about space; it's claustrophobic because it takes place on a small ship in the vastness of infinity, infinite at least in relation to our ability to conceive of finitude, space, and this contrast makes the space of the ship infinitely smaller. And yet the ship is still relatively enormous in relation to the human body, and the human body is still relatively small in relation to the alien body of the alien monster that newly inhabits and terrorizes the ship, and so the ship, which is a place, becomes space, because it has been defamiliarized, newly estranged by the alienizing presence of the alien who may be hiding in any area of the ship, the alien who conquers space by being able to become space, itself, who can change its shape and hide anywhere, it's unnoticeable as long as it chooses to escape notice, and yet it invests all of space with its possible lethal presence. Every moment in that movie spans an eternity, because of all the anxiety of it. Aliens, the woman continues, wiping the steam off her glasses with a bar napkin and peering at them, not at me through them, is an action adventure film. There is a whole brood of aliens and a whole cadre of military crew and each member of each race is expendable, it's no longer a dramatization of the struggle to survive but a staging of the cheapness of life, total war and total carnage. It's a grand theater of war. That's James Cameron's specialty, the scale of the large, which makes drama small. That's Aliens. Ridley Scott works more minimalistically, and so the human and emotional drama is enormous. That's Alien. The Iliad is Aliens, but I don't know that I can say The Odyssey is Alien. That's my current quandary, she says, and looks up at me for the first time. Her eyes are bloodshot, her brain hair, the brown hair over her naked brain, is mousy, her complexion pale. She is wearing a cream-colored fur coat, and underneath it a black and gray sweater with reindeer on it, or the shadowy outlines of reindeer. It's not even cold in Santa Cruz, or in the bar, but I guess it is raining. But it only began raining while I was in the bar. But she's not even wet. I can only think of lists of things that are not, negative lists. I know this about myself. When I try to think of what is, of what exists, it's always only ludicrous guesswork, chimeras of the real and the unreal, but that's only apparent to others.

This quandary is why you're crying at the bar? I say.

No, she says. I'm crying from a catastrophe, not a quandary. A quandary is something that can be solved. I'm crying from something that is total ruination, she says.

Why does the Odyssey have to be Alien? I say. Can't it be something else?

It would be neater, it would fit into a pre-established category, even if that category is arbitrary, a personal category, a personal alphabet, it would make me feel better, she says, if I could just say The Iliad is James Cameron's Aliens, and The Odyssey is Ridley Scott's Alien. It would be easier to write about, she says.

Why can't The Odyssey be Alien, I say.

Because the only thing The Odyssey and Alien have in common, really, is that they follow one main character, Odysseus and Ripley, respectively, she says. Otherwise they have nothing in common; The Odyssey has more in common with the Iliad than Alien has in common with Aliens. The Odyssey isn't cramped, there's no narrative-long confinement to one space, there's confinement to many different spaces which, ironically, implies movement and freedom, throughout the whole world in this case, and there are huge battles, also, or at least skirmishes, and there's not just one monster that becomes the negative foil to the main character, Odysseus. The enemy is the whole world. The enemy is the gods.

Why don't you just bend the criteria a little, then, I say. Can't the Odyssey and the Iliad both just be James Cameron movies? What if the Iliad is Aliens by James Cameron, and the Odyssey is Avatar by James Cameron?

She starts crying again, but this time takes her glasses off first. This time too it's not sobs or anything guttural, but tears sliding out her eyes. Her tears are a visual experience. She's looking at me, although often I haven't been looking at her. I can only look at someone when they're not looking at me. It's a game of chicken. I'm a coward. I look at someone until they look at me, and then I turn my head. This time though I turn to her when I say the word Avatar, and she turns to me, too, and the tears slide out as the glasses slide off, or she slides them off with her fingers, whatever. Maybe, she says, you can help me with my other quandary.

I thought you said it was a catastrophe, I say.

I'm a catastrophe, she says, not my problem. Hell isn't other people, she says. Hell is Alien, by Homer.

What's your quandtastrophe, I say.

I'm writing my dissertation on the sestina, she says, do you know it?

No, I say.

Maybe you can't help me, she says. She slides down to the bar again, her elbows splaying out on the ledge like seal fins on a rock. What is it you do? she says.

I'm in real estate, I say.

You definitely can't help me, she says.

What's a sestina, I say.

The sestina is a poetic form, she says. It's maybe the most difficult to write in, difficult because the most repetitive and tedious. Each stanza is six lines, and each line ends with one predetermined word. In the next stanza, the lines end with the same predetermined words, but in a different order. You switch the order of the word-ending lines depending on their positioning in the previous stanza. If the sixth and last line of the first stanza ends in the word bluejay, for example, then the first line of the next stanza will end in the word bluejay. Next, if the first line of the first stanza ends in the word blowjob, the second line of the second stanza will end with the word blowjob. If the penultimate, sorry, the fifth line of the first stanza ends in the word Betelgeuse, then the third line of the second stanza will end in the

18

word Betelgeuse. If the second line of the first stanza ends in the word Bojack, the fourth line of the second stanza ends in the word Bojack. If the fourth line of the first stanza ends in the word broadjump, the fifth line of the second stanza ends in the word broadjump. If the third line of the first stanza ends in the word breadjoy, then the sixth and final line of the new second stanza will end on the word breadjoy.

Even though breadjoy isn't a word, I say.

In a poem, the woman says, whatever assemblage of language is phonemically sound is a word.

Is phonemically sound a pun, I say.

Yes, she says.

I would like to read that poem, I say.

I would like to write it, she says. The next stanza will be organized according to the same logic, until there are six full stanzas. Finally, the seventh stanza is three lines. The three lines in this case do not need to follow the pattern of the previous stanzas' end line; they couldn't, after all, being only three. Nonetheless the three lines must now incorporate all six of the poem's repeating words.

So the poem could conceivably end:

> Bojack's breadjoy is
> to Betelgeuse's broadjump
> as a blowjob's to a bluejay

I say, marking off the endlines aloud by pointing up my thumb, and then pointing up my pointer, and then my middle finger, so I'm holding three fingers aloft.

Yes, the woman says. You could certainly end the poem that way, in fact it would be innovative. The sestina is a very old form but it isn't ancient, maybe half a millennium old. It's a French form. It drives writers insane and, in many creative writing classes, teachers will teach a sestina as a sort of hazing ritual, a way of testing to see if you, the aspiring writer, know what you're getting into with poetry. The redundancy of it, the emptiness, the plodding, the tedium, the stiltedness. Most people don't write in sestinas for this reason, and it's not widely used because most people don't see the point in doing it, the function. On the other hand some of the most beautiful poems I have ever read are sestinas. I have discovered in the sestina form a form of devotion rarely seen in other forms; why else recycle the same words unless through an act of devotion? To turn rote repetition into chanting devotion, to turn reuse into reverence. These same recalled words must be used in different ways, with different syntactical functions and different contextualizations, to keep the sestina fresh and turning. You use the word "jack" as an end line word, for example, and you discover all its potential, or at least six points of potential: Jack or Jill, jack of the game jacks, the second half of carjack, jacked up on coffee, jack- / fruit enjambed to the next line, etc. These verbal transformations herald for me, or are metaphorical for, the same sorts of transformations we seek to find in life, the word becomes another word as a person meets their Other and is changed by and even perhaps into their Other, the human life is halved and metamorphosed as they turn / to something or someone else (fruiting) – here the woman pantomimes parentheses by turning to me, taking the pointer finger of each hand, and drawing in the air vertical semicircles as she says "fruiting" – the queering of the line and of the word, all of these potentialities are expressed by the form of the sestina itself, it's primrose promise of literally literary revolution. It's sexy, she says, and smiles. She's maybe lost, or transformed. I've been writing about this for 8 years, she says, and her smile drops.

What are you calling the dissertation? I say.

Sex Tina, she says. That's the problem.

That's the funniest thing I've ever heard, I say, and I think it is, actually, the funniest thing I've ever heard. I can't tell whether it's brilliant or dumb, so I think it must be brilliant. Why is that the problem, I say.

Because someone just came out with a book of sestinas last month called Sexy Tinas, she says, and more tears slide out her eyes. I don't know how it's possible but there's a tear sliding down the rim of one monocle of her glasses. One circle? Half of her glasses? I realize I don't know how to refer to half of one's glasses. To her glass? I think this as I watch the transparent tear on the transparent medium. This was my niche, she says, no one was writing about this, and now this comes out, and the author is being written about in the New York Times as revolutionary, as radically reinventing and reinvesting an old form, and it has all the same themes as the ones I am writing about, immanence, transcendence, queer lyrics, radical ruptures, and now everyone will think I copied her, even though I've worked on this for nearly a decade now, not only because it's about the same subject, but because it has *the same name*. And this bizarro double of me, this binary star Betelgeuse, has discovered the only name possible for the book – even if it resembles a joke, and maybe because it resembles a joke, *it has to be the name of the book*, it can't be any other name, the name of the form demands it – and now I can't call it that. Now my book has no name.

I look at the woman who looks ahead at the mirror on the back of the bar's backing, reflecting her stare back at her. Then I look at the mirror and I see in my periphery my reflection, and see in my main focus her reflection. There's a reflected baby foot high above us; I feel a tightening in my chest, suddenly, and the urge also suddenly to shit my pants. I turn myself on my stool to face her. Hey, I say. What's your name?

She meets me almost as quickly, turns her torso for the first time, too, towards me. Her anxiety seems to mimic mine; it doesn't feel authentic, I think, it's mine, I think, it's mine. Give it back, I think. She puts on a smile. Like it's a hat she's trying on. She says, My name's Danny. What's yours? she says.

Danny the 50 year-old punk rocker and Danny the 12 year-old Madonna fan are playing pool together in the background of the bar and the background of my life, though now I foreground them in my listening.

Hey man can I try on that scarf? says Danny

This is a special scarf, Danny says.

Are you hiding a hickey or something? says Danny

I wish, Danny says, I just broke up with my girlfriend. Actually honestly she broke up with me, she thought I was cheating on her. I don't know how to not run my mouth, I guess, I kept talking about the girl that sells me these scarves, and eventually she was like, Enough! You want me to start selling you scarves? Will you like me better then? So I guess these scarves stopped me from getting hickeys altogether. But we weren't getting hickeys anyway, we weren't really sleeping together. I don't know why women are so jealous. I've been buying a lot more scarves lately though.

Hey man I'm sorry to hear that. But it's your shot, I just got one of yours in, says Danny.

That's the 8-ball. You got the 8-ball in. You ever played pool before? Now it's no one's shot, Danny says.

Oh, says Danny. Good game. What's your name, man?

My name's Danny, Danny says. What's your

name dude?

My name's Danny, says Danny. Good to meet you, Danny.

Nice meeting you, Danny, Danny says. Hey, you ever heard of the Madonna Complex? I was talking to that guy over there about it, he had some helpful things to say about it. You're going through a breakup and seem to know women well, I feel like you could help me out, too.

Yeah? says Danny. I was talking to that guy, too, but he didn't have much to say when I talked. What's his name?

He told me, Danny says, but I forget.

Yeah, says Danny, me too.

I only half-hear the two of them, but I catch them exchanging names, or name. Danny said he never plays pool with other people, but here he is playing pool with Danny. Maybe it's because he's still playing pool with himself, nominally, Danny is playing pool with Danny. I'm surprised there are three people with names that sound like "Danny" in the bar, I say it like that because I don't know how they spell it. Probably D-A-N-N-Y, but maybe the woman I'm talking to spells it Dani, for example, and I knew a girl in elementary school named "Davni." The v was silent. Once I asked her about it, after college, when I moved to New York, and saw her at a bar with a high school friend, and she said, when I was a kid I told my parents I wanted a v in my name. I wanted a v in my name really really bad. So they let me have a v in my name. And it's been there ever since. I've never changed my mind, or my name.

I look at Dani, or Davni, or Danny, and I say

Do you spell your name with an i?

No, Danny says, that would be crazy.

I don't know how that would be crazy at all, I think to myself. But who else would I think it to. Danny as a name for a girl I feel is kind of uncharacteristic. Or untraditional. Uncommon, that's the word I'm looking for. Dani is the more common variant for women's names, I think, with that sound. Why would that be crazy? I think it's crazy to call it crazy. I change the subject.

Why don't you just keep the same name? I say. Just call it Sex Tina, too.

And she says But then we'd have the same name.

And I say Yeah I know, but what does it mean to have the same name? Why does it matter?

And she says Well one of us must be copying the other, is what it means. It means one of us came first.

And I say But one of us is always copying the other. One of us always came first. That's true regardless.

And she says I don't think you understand copyright, or issues of aesthetic appropriation and authority.

And I say Why don't you put a v in it?

And she says What?

And I say Why don't you put a v in it? Name it Sexvy Tivna?

And she says But it's already named Sexy Tina

And I say No but spell it S-E-X-V-N-Y T-I-V-N-A

And she says So I call my book Sexvy Tivna?

And I say No, call it Sexvy Tivna. The v is silent. It's there but only you know it's there, except in writing.

And she says But it's a book. It's all writing.

And I say So the secret is aloud, then. No one knows how to say it.

And she says I don't know what you're talking about.

And I say Whavt doves vit mattver. But I say "Whavt doves vit matter" with three silent v's, so she doesn't know I've said it, unless I spelled it out for her, but I'm not going to spell it out for her if she doesn't ask me to spell it out for her, and how could she ask that if she doesn't know there's something to ask at all, if the secret is itself secret?

And she says What if the v's are invisible, too.

And I say I don't know what you're talking about.

And she says I'e secretiely diied out inisible 's.

And I say Call it The elet Underground.

And she says You're ery perceptie.

But I don't know if I'm perceptive. I don't know if we're doing this at all, if we're sharing this at all, or if I'm perceiving what I think she's doing, because everything sounds the same, but I'm imagining we're reading something aloud that has been written with invisible v's, and I can't see if there's something to see, and everything sounds the same. I look up and think, Baby shoes, never worn. Making feet for baby shoes, I think. And then I shudder. And then I say, How do you spell your name.

And she says What?

And I say how do you spell your name, Danny?

And she says Danny is spelled the way Danny is spelled.

And I say Sometimes people spell things different, like my friend Davni with a v.

And she says But Danny is spelled pretty straightforward.

The bartender is dawdling on her phone in the back corner by the broken ID scanner. I wave at her and I ask her if I can borrow a pen. She hands me a yellow push-pen that says TARMAC on the body of it. I thank her and order another whiskey. As she walks towards the Buffalo Trace bottle I take a white cocktail napkin from a square stand of them, and I hand it and the pen to Danny, and I say Will you write your name?

Danny writes her name in all caps. It is cursive, but I can't type cursive on a computer, and it is all-caps, which I can type. See? Danny says. How else would you spell it?

M-O-L-L-Y says the napkin.

Danny, she says. Daaaaanny, Danny says. You want to play Hangman? Danny says.

I have an idea. I look at my phone and it's 8:00. My idea will work.

I have an idea, I say to Danny. Will you hold my seat? I'll be right back.

Okay, says Danny, and slurs her Okay. It's really hard to slur Okay, but not at the Jury Room, I've come to decide.

I wobble out of my stool and say to the bartender I'll be right back. The bartender looks at me and smiles and waves and says Goodbye, as if "I'll be right back" is the way most Jury Room patrons say goodbye. She clears my glass. I wonder if I will come back, I think this is an opportunity to leave, actually, that I'm being granted, it's a second chance, I never ever have to come back here. But I've also had my idea and I think it's a good idea and it will help me find out some things. Although it might also just introduce new questions that I can't answer. If that's the case hopefully I'll have another idea. Sometimes I think of questions and answers, of mysteries and revelations, as the play between bacterial infections and antibiotics. Eventually the bacteria grows resistant to the antibiotics and you start taking more antibiotics, or new stronger antibiotics. But scientific developments take longer than natural developments. Scientific developments require money, laboratory conditions, testing, approval from people in lab coats. Bacteria doesn't even have to fuck. I don't even know what bacteria has to do, but I don't think it even has to fuck. It's like the Madonna, but bacteria doesn't need god. And fucking takes only slightly longer than dying. It depends on what you consider the starting point of dying. I guess it also depends on what you consider the starting point of fucking. If you follow someone on Instagram who eventually becomes your husband, was that part of fucking? The beginning point depends on knowledge of the end point to be considered a beginning point, so it becomes the beginning only after the end point. The end point really is the beginning. Is that a Smashing Pumpkins lyric? Fucking is following. Fucking follows following. I walk into the Dollar Tree.

There's a tree-shaped mint decal on the entrance. The door jingles with bells I can't see. There's mistletoe at the top of the door. I wonder if this is where Adam and Eve went after they learned their own and each other's names and death and went north by northwest of Eden. Sometimes I don't think god banished Adam and Eve because he was mad at them, because they ate all his pink ladies, or what. I just think, like a cat crawling under a house to die privately, god didn't want Adam and Eve to watch him die. Maybe when they ate the pink ladies it didn't give them the knowledge of death, but god watching them learned about death, and started dying. Or maybe Adam and Eve were just god splitting, like a bacterium. Maybe god was just the process of the two of them splitting and then they left Eden and god started singing 'I think we're alone now,' and died. There's a whole line of Pez dispensers at the register. One of them is Chester the Cheetah, one of them is Richard Nixon, one of them is Mao Zedung, one of them is Peppa Pig, one of them is Michael Jordan, one of them is Danny Trejo, one of them is Danny Devito, one of them is Danny Glover, one of them is St. Denis, one of them is Dennis Rodman, one of them is Don Trump and one of them is Stormy Daniels. In the glass case below them are ice cream sandwiches. The cashier says Can I help you? I wonder, also, if he can help me. In a box above his head on a shelf are cartoon drawings of smiling dinosaurs and the whole affair is called JIGGLE DIGS.

What are JIGGLE DIGS? I say.

What? he says.

What are those JIGGLE DIGS above your head? I say.

He turns around. He has white whiskery hair on his nape. He looks up. He re-arranges his glasses on the bridge of his nose, he plucks the glasses with his thumbs and pointers of both hands to both lenses and moves them a centimeter away from his eyes, like the glasses are actually two pairs of monocles. I don't know, he says. Do you want to look at the box?

Do you sell those MY NAME IS stickers? I say.

What? he says.

Do you sell those stickers that are like name tags but they're stickers you stick on your shirt, and on each is typed MY NAME IS in all-caps, but then there's a blank line, and you write your own name on it before you put it on, then you put it on, and you wear them at business meetings and things.

Oh, you mean the MY NAME IS stickers? he says.

Yes, I say.

Yeah, we have some left, he says. You know, I don't display them but I've always sold them, for twenty years, and no one ever, ever buys them, but just today I've had a few people buying some. What's that about? Is there a business convention in town? It's pretty late for a business convention, he says, looking to his left at a mounted clock whose minute arm is the outstretched arm of Dan Marino, and above the twelve in cerulean blue is printed MIAMI DOLPHINS. It's weird when a clock is vintage, I think. Like time is itself old.

Maybe, I say, I don't know. I just want to know people's names.

Why don't you just ask people's names, the cashier says. It's cheaper.

What's your name? I say.

Why do you wanna know? he says.

See what I mean? I say.

What? he says.

I'll buy twenty of them, I say. Actually, twenty-one if you'll fill one out and wear one.

They're 50 cents apiece, he says.

That's fine, I say.

I pay with the tap on my phone. He hands me twenty cards. I watch my phone die after I've paid, and I stare at my phone. I stare at its corpse. There's nothing I can do now. When I look up I see the cashier is wearing a name tag. HELLO, MY NAME IS FRANKIE.

Thanks, Frankie, I say.

What? he says.

Thanks, I say, and walk out with the cards in my jacket pocket. I walk into the Jury Room. There's a lot of people here now, like they've grown from the seats. My bar seat is taken, but Danny's is empty, except for a napkin with a hangman game drawn on it. The hangman figure is totally drawn, and only three of five letters are filled in:

_ L _ I D

Did Danny leave? Did I play this with her and forget? Did she play this alone? Is it a message to me? Is this finished or unfinished? Is this a game or a code? Are letters missing or are letters invisible? Do you want a drink? the bartender asks me.

I can answer this question, I think. I'll have another round, I say.

Another round of what? she says.

I'll have a whiskey on the rocks, I say.

Okay, she says. When she returns with my drink she says That'll be six dollars. It was only five dollars an hour ago, I think. Inflation is fast, I think. I hand her a ten and a sticker and I say This is for you, too.

What the fuck is this about? she says, holding the MY NAME IS sticker.

Honestly, I have the same question, I say. From the softening look she gives me, it must look like I'm about to cry.

The bartender hands me my glass of whiskey; to the side of the glass facing me she's stuck the sticker, and filled it out so it says HELLO, MY NAME IS WHISKEY. My name's Danny, she says, but you can call me Danny.

Hi, Danny, I say.

I'd ask your name but from your sticker I guess I don't have to. Nice to meet you, Danny. Are you new in town? I've never seen you here before.

I have not written DANNY on the sticker, but FRANKIE, to see if the outside world has any power here. I guess the laws of the Jury Room are different. I wonder if it's like the MYSTERY SPOT, which I've never been to, but you see it in black font on bright yellow bumper stickers on cars all over the place; the other day I saw a car entirely plastered in those stickers, so it resembled Dick Tracy's car, if Dick Tracy's car is yellow. I think it's yellow. The MYSTERY SPOT is supposed to be a location that somehow suffers from a gravitational aberration, you try to stand straight up but instead you're at a 45 degree angle, but you feel as stable as always, you're not going to fall down, and balls roll up declines, and balls roll down declines, this is what I've heard but I've never been there because I just moved here and because I don't care. I wonder if the Jury Room is the same for names, you just can't say names aloud other than Danny. But then I remember Danny saying

Sexy Tina, and saying James Cameron, and saying Ridley Scott, etc. But those names are inventions and celebrities, and celebrities are inventions, too, and Homer wasn't even one real person, just a conglomeration of ancient oral unknowns gathered under one name. Do Danny's here have friends they can recall that are not named Danny? What happens when they're outside the bar, or beyond this block, is the curse lifted? Can I say other names aloud? But I'm at least aware of the possibility that I can't say other names aloud, and they don't seem aware.

Frankie, I say.

What did you say? the bartender says.

Frankie, I say.

What do you want? the bartender says.

What? I say.

Why do you keep saying my name? the bartender says.

I have an idea. Surely you must be joking, I say.

And the bartender says, No, I'm very serious...and don't call me Danny.

Have you ever seen Airplane II? I say. In my head I said it with Roman Numerals, I wrote it in my head this way. And then I wrote it in my head as Airplane Danny Danny.

Yes, says the bartender, the one where they're flying into the sun?

Yes that's the one, I say.

It's funny you ask, the bartender says. I was in the sauna the other day, at a spa, the bartender says. It was a Korean spa and they have all these rooms with different temperatures and different names. There's like 5 of them. There's an order you're supposed to enter them but I don't know the order: one room is freezing and there are stalactites hanging from the ceiling and snow packed onto the surrounding walls. It's weird, I don't know if you're supposed to enter it first or last, or third, but third wouldn't make sense, it's the coldest room and I feel like extremes fall on extremes, you know, on ends, first or last. Anyway the first really hot room I entered was called the Clay Room, it's about 135 degrees, it says it in neon lights outside the entrance. The glass of the door is hot, the marble floor is hot, and then there's a sort of straw mat you lie down on and a slightly warm pillow that feels like cardboard, and you stare up onto a ceiling that's covered in what appear to be small stumps of petrified wood, they're charred black, it's very calming because it looks natural and it looks unnatural at the same time. And I lie down and I'm so pleasantly toasty but I'm thinking if it were one degree warmer, if it were one-tenth of a degree warmer, I'd start to panic. And then I start thinking of the movie Airplane 2. And I think, were those people experiencing a room with a similar temperature to mine? What if the temperature was actually cooler than mine; sure the temperature ought to have been rising as they were getting nearer and nearer the sun, but what if in all that it was a slow increase, and they never even reached the temperature of what to me was an incredibly hot room. Was it just the fact of increase, and the fear that that increase in temperature would never stop? Was it because they knew they were approaching the sun? What if they got on an airplane that was supposed to be that hot, from the get-go, what then? Would they complain it wasn't hot enough? The bartender takes a shot of tequila. She opens a little black tray and picks out a lime, and tears into it with her teeth. Lime juice squirts into my eye. It strikes me she's very close to me right now. Her nails are painted a striking white, but on each nail is a pearl-shaped and pearl-colored stud, a protruding ball the size of a pea. How is she bartending? I wonder.

Your nails are cool, I say. They don't get in the way of bartending? Like the citrus, or the sanitizer fluid, none of that gunks it up or breaks it down?

You've bartended before, she says, and pours me a shot glass of Fernet.

I've barbacked, I say.

I like barebacking, too, she says, and winks at me.

Yeah it's punishing work but it's satisfying, I say, pretending I didn't see or hear her. Maybe it is good to be Danny here, I think. Maybe it is good to have no accountability here, it's not that I'm anonymous at this bar, I'm just nymous. Maybe all bars are like this, I think. Maybe all rooms are like this, I think. Maybe a room is just a metaphor for an entire universe, an outdoor universe, and human consciousness is just a patio, I think.

If you want to know a secret, Danny says, I'll tell you it, Danny says. I think to myself how in late antiquity the ancient Egyptians had priests whose sole function was to guard the secret of the universe; their entire job rested on not divulging that secret. The belief was that if they did divulge the secret of the universe, the universe would crumble, it would end. Maybe, I think, one of them told a very very very very very very small portion of that secret, and a very very very very small portion of the universe crumbled, and that small portion is called The Jury Room, I think.

Tell me, Danny, I say to the bartender.

Well, she says, if you were a bareback (she winks again) you know about the three-basin system.

For washing glasses? I say. Yeah, I say. First basin soap water and scrub brushes, second basin warm water, and third basin water and sanitizing fluid.

Second basin cold water, the bartender corrects me, but yes. She leans in closer: I replaced the sanitizing fluid with bleach. Bleach doesn't affect my nails, she whispers, except that they become even whiter.

That's why your nails are the color of snow, I say. Every part of your nails is the color of ploughed, pure-driven snow, I say.

That's right, she says.

And that's worth slowly but surely poisoning us? Are you joking?

I'm not joking, she says. And don't call me Danny.

What? I say.

And don't call me Danny, she says. I'm joking.

Surely, Danny, I say.

You think that whiskey isn't killing you? the bartender says.

I'd like to pick my poison, I say.

Then go to Alcoholics Anonymous, she says, Danny boy.

Being called Danny upsets me; when she turns around I peel the FRANKIE sticker off my shirt. Suddenly I hear "Danny boy" again, but this time behind me. I turn around but I don't see anyone's mouth matching the sound. Then I hear it again, then again, then again. It's singing, no one is saying it, it's singing. Danny was singing it, too. The track is stuck. Fucking jukebox, says Danny, and walks over and smacks it. The song stops skipping, it resumes its normal, neutral course. Danny walks over to a new customer who has entered. She looks bored; her nails look bored. They're not reflective though they're metal. Maybe she was joking about the bleach, too. She never specified what she was joking about. "The purpose of the joke, you see, was,'" she didn't say. I see there are blobby pink stains on her jeans; bleach stains. I walk over to the jukebox. The current play is Tubthumping by Chumbawumba. The next play in the queue is Do It Again by Steely Dan.

Did you know Chumbawumba was an anarchopunk band? a guy behind me asks. I turn around. He is taller than me, but I am not very tall, and he is ganglier than me, and I am sort of gangly. His teeth are horrible brown nubs, and it seems like there are rows of them, and his lips are thin pink excrescences out his face. I always look at mouths when people talk. I wonder if it's sexual, people say it's always sexual to watch someone's mouth when someone's talking, and maybe that's true, but I always do it. It's not hard for me to imagine anyone fucking, I've been to mass and watched nuns orate and my mind works out them giving oration to bent over priests shuddering 'alleilujahs in the dark. But mostly when I look at mouths I think of people's diets, what they eat, if they smoke, how they frown, their laugh lines, I think about if they're mouth-breathers, what their resting face is when they watch a movie, whether they murmur when they read, if they smile when they receive texts, I feel like I can see all of these things when I look at a mouth, I look for the traces, I drink Buffalo trace, I wonder if anyone's traced my phone before, the currents that leave a char on the face and mark it with evidence of all the minutiae of a life's habits. This guy looks like a Jackson, but I know better.

No I never knew that, I say.

It makes sense if you think about it, Danny says. They wrote this song as a joke, but the joke became famous and it's all we know of their music, all the serious stuff got eclipsed by the joke, and now they're just a joke. But listen to the lyrics: "I get knocked down, but I get up again. And you're never gonna keep me down," Danny pumps his fists into the air, both of them, and I'm afraid he's going to hit the ceiling. He's affected a British drawl, too. The lyrics repeat throughout the song, you can't even keep the lyrics down, he says.

They just get up again, I say.

Exactly, he says. It's a metaphor for the revolutionary spirit, he says, but also about the sleepiness of the proletariat, drugged by drink and never able to realize itself. But it's also hardy, resilient, so it's always there, you can always hope.

That's the other side of revolution, I say. It just revolves. It does the same thing over and over again. It goes around and around and around, I say. Sorry, am I in your way? Did you want to use the jukebox?

No, Danny says, I just don't have anywhere to sit, and I'm waiting for my girlfriend to show up. She's never been here before and I feel like she'll be scared if she doesn't see me first thing, he says. He scans the entranceway, but the entranceway is blocked from view anyway, there's a narrow corridor that's blocked in velvet curtains at an immediate 90 degree turn you have to pass through right after passing through the front door, so people just pop into view with no warning. But what kind of warning would there be anyway? I think. Here I come to save the day?

I think.

Do you come here a lot then? I say.

Yeah I'm from here, born and raised, Danny says.

I never understood that phrase, I say.

What do you mean? Danny says.

Well it's not like you were born *or* raised, it has to be both. So it's kind of superfluous, I say. I was also born and raised, I say.

Yes but I was born and raised *here*, Danny says. All the formative events of my life, including being formed in the first place, took place in Santa Cruz, Danny says, and that's the point, to drive that home.

To drive home that this is home, I say. And your girlfriend isn't from here? I say.

No she's from LA and she lives there, too, Danny says.

Born and raised? I say.

Actually, Danny says, she was born in LA, then was raised largely in Taiwan, and then came back to LA to attend USC to study film. So that sort of disproves your point about being born and raised, Danny says, and flashes his teeth.

Your argument has teeth, I say.

What? Danny says.

Your argument has teeth, I says.

Mm, Danny says. He says it with his mouth closed. It's a way of saying "oh" without opening one's mouth. He must feel self-conscious about his teeth because I've drawn attention to them through a metaphor, and he must feel angry at me, but he's not sure if that anger is earned or legitimate. But it is earned and it is legitimate; it is what I did. I've been expert in this since I was a barback, making comments to customers to make them slightly uncomfortable, revealing something about their insecurities that I have noticed, but without revealing that I have noticed it. It's a kind of spamming; is this message intended for me? I'm not actively seeking penis enlargement, but penis enlargement ads have found me, and why? Does it know something about me? I check my spam box multiple times a day. Maybe I'm waiting for something, maybe I'm afraid the Gmail algorithm has misrecognized something as banal or irrelevant or scammy, but what, I wonder, if I've missed something direly important? What if the message is so important that it's rerouted to spam purely because the import of my general mail is generally low, and in fact everything I receive in the general mailbox is banal, irrelevant, spam? Maybe the spam folder isn't the id of the psyche of my inbox, maybe it's the superego, pure message, maybe Way.com's subject line "Woof-tastic savings on National Puppy Day!" enciphers within itself the secrets of human communication, all of desire, the nucleus of interpersonal interaction, the tao of the Dow Jones, what we kow tow to when we bow wow wag before our money masters, paycheck to paycheck. I need to start monitoring my drinking, I think to myself.

Hey, man, what the fuck are you staring at? says Danny.

What? I say.

You've been blank-eyed gazing at I-don't-know-the-fuck-what for a minute now. You trying to get faded? Danny says. His fists are clenched at his sides. I see a trickle of sweat run down his beanie, and stop at a vein in his temple.

No, I say. No, I just smoked some weed, I say. Sorry, I was distracted by your teeth. They're really horrible. They remind me of Shane McGowan's, from The Pogues. I think he has replacement teeth at this point. He's a genius. Do you think he ever listened to Chumbawumba?

Danny's fists unclench. Haha, he laughs, and bares his teeth more openly. Sorry, man. Or fuck you, man, I don't know. I'm faded, too. But I have a chip on my shoulder about my teeth, he says, and now that you've said something about it, I don't have to worry about it. I brush every day but it doesn't do anything; I don't floss, but I don't think that matters. I drink a lot, he says, and polishes off his Modelo, but so do you, clearly, you bug-eyed weirdo, and your teeth don't look like this. Me and my girlfriend are open; it's fine, I get to see other women, it's interesting, but it's not what I want. Sometimes I wonder if it's because of my teeth. Like she wants to run her tongue over teeth that don't feel like Braille, he says. His eyes become glossy, blind-seeming. I admire the imagery of that, or the anti-imagery, the blindness of it. I always wished I knew Braille, so I could read in the dark. Or I could fumble with a book in my bag at the bar and read and no one would know it. But then they'd think I was jerking off, probably. How long have I been thinking? It creates noticeable lags in conversation, it seems, that others notice but I don't notice.

I do, says Danny, and I think he's about to reply to my thought, and maybe he has, but he continues, think Shane McGowan listened to Chumbawumba.

What's your favorite Pogues song, I say.

Danny! he shouts. A slim and blonde and pale woman walks over to us, taller even than Danny, and they kiss in front of the jukebox. This is Danny, he says to me, and Danny reaches out her hand. Danny, this is, well, shit, I don't even know your name. You don't even know mine! I'm Danny, he says to me.

Nice to meet you, Danny says to me. Who are you? she says.

Yeah! Danny says, I don't even know who you are! We were just talking about the Pogues, and my shitty teeth, and how I think you're not into me because of them.

Shut the fuck up, Danny, Danny says, and pulls Danny by the scruff of his hair, which I can't see through his beanie, a thorough clench, and lashes her tongue across his teeth. Danny laughs, and so does Danny. I love your teeth, she says, they have character. I've named each little one, she says. What were you saying about the Pogues? I love the Pogues, she says and laughs. I wonder what she's named the teeth, until, on second thought, I don't.

This guy had just asked me which Pogues song was my favorite song. Usually it's this one song off Peace and Love, but I'm too drunk to remember the name of it right now. So maybe it's Danny Boy. Maybe Chumbawumba is quoting that song in Tubthumping. I've never thought about that. What's yours? he says to me. What's your name even? he says to me.

I'm too drunk to remember the name of it, of me right now, I say.

You're a drunk little parrot, Danny says to me. Danny born or raised in LA.

Danny asks me what I do. I tell her I'm in publishing, I'm the head of commissioning, of acquisitions of new titles. Danny's a first AC, or Assistant Camera, alternatively called a focus puller, her job is to maintain sharpness of focus on whatever object or person is being filmed at the time, a dog, a piece of lint, a serial number, a thought bubble, a samurai, a hummingbird, a daffodil, a fistful of basmati rice hurled into the air, the cloud behind the air behind the jasmine cloud that is a cloud if focus is not pulled, a bullseye, a furrowed brow, a Pepsi can, a Coke can, a Danielle Steele book jacket, a Jack Daniels bottle, a bloody elbow, Stonehenge, a PowerPoint slideshow of all these things ahead of the blurred bored crown of a student in a classroom watching. She wears a patch that says AC: Always Crying, on a jean jacket. A Nikon camera is slung over her shoulder, her hair is piles of curls of buoyant red, she wears a tight-fitting gold necklace with a big opalescent pearl settled in the center on her clavicle I find I want to touch. She laughs easy and melts into a pair of arms, the knees below her mauve skirt buckling smoothly. Velcro seatbelt, I think. Hardcore headrest, I think.

Danny's father is a manager at Pizza Hut and this, not ethnicity or heritage or business or politics, is what brought her for so long to Taiwan. I remember hearing that in mainland China Pizza Hut is fine dining, I don't know if it's the same in Taiwan. She's just watched the Darron Aranofsky movie The Whale – what's the director's name again she says, Danny Aranofsky? – with Brendan Frasier, and hated it. What's the fucking point? she says. Why does it try to convince us so much, optically even, with that floor shot to make him look huger, that he's fucking disgusting? And then his death is due to his being fucking disgusting, and maybe his fucking disgusting state has him crush his daughter? They call him, fucking, The Whale? Do they think this is a lesson in fat-shaming? There's no lesson in it, it's just fat-shaming porn, she says. I think she's right.

Danny is reading Outline by Rachel Cusk, Horror in Architecture by Joshua Comaroff. She doesn't like mushrooms, she loves camo patterns, she tries to go to Bass Pro Shop once a month, to see the latest styles. She thinks the Outline series by Rachel Cusk is interesting, because it reads like nonfiction. The narrator is so nondescript, submits her personality to a cast of other personalities that are presented more like cameos than characters, meandering in to fill space with their words on their lives and their egos and their particular ways of talking, so the narrator seems more like a camo background for these other talking heads, a stage and, Danny says, why shouldn't it be autobiographical, then? What's the need for an invented main character if that character's flatness acts as a landscape on which other characters can walk, stretch, be in their bodies? It makes her think how fiction is flimsy, nominal at best, and that the only thing required, often by law, by the threat of lawsuits, is name changes. You meet someone in real life and you change their name to something else and the best way to fictionalize them is to accurately portray them, their outline, to breathe life in them anew, a recirculation of blood. It's not invention. It's translation. But translation is about changing the names of words. The meanings are the same, Danny says, just the names of the things that transmit the same meanings aren't, Danny says. It was just my birthday and I turned 30. Am I supposed to be tired all the time now? I love Danny, Danny says, because he gave me his heart. He made me a book, he sewed it and bound it himself, in it were all the things he loves about me, it's like he gave me his heart, Danny says. My childhood friend Danny, Danny says, said that that's the gift we all want from our partners, their heart, for them to give us their heart. I love Danny's heart, and Danny loves my heart. He has my heart, Danny says.

I got pretty good at Taiwanese Mandarin while I was there, made flashcards of characters and read them aloud to myself while on the bus to the city, passengers would ask me what I was doing, in Mandarin, I would respond, in Mandarin. But mostly I was listening, Danny says. I noticed people, I found many people beautiful, but I rarely fall in love. When I do it takes up everything in me, Danny says. It takes time. It's stressful. But it's not stressful with Danny, he doesn't ask anything of me. My Mandarin is bad now. They say speaking another language is like riding a bike, you've learned to ride a bike and you don't ride for years and then you get back on it and after a couple of hours it's like you'd never stopped riding it, that's not true with Taiwanese, Danny says, in America. It's more like riding a unicycle. There aren't that many unicycles around to practice on, even in LA, she says and laughs. It's the most beautiful laugh I've ever seen.

Heard. I don't see anyone else in the room, they're all blurry, even Danny, whose arm is around her, but to me it's just like Danny has three hands, one that's an outgrowth on her shoulder, so only two arms. I could be in love with Danny, I think. It would be so easy to be in love with Danny; does that mean I'm already in love? I ask myself. I imagine us meeting in LA, I live in LA and I'm an actor, Danny is an actor, we're in a movie together, a horror movie, I'm the killer and she's the killed, I'm in a red smoking jacket, the kind that waiters wear at steakhouses, she's holding a steak knife, maybe she's the one that kills me, though I'm the murderer. M-E-A-T is tattooed on the knuckles of her left hand. M-A-T-E is tattooed on the knuckles of her right. It's so easy to imagine another life, Danny's in a night shift, it's translucent, she has black panties, I'm in my red smoking jacket, I'm a waiter that's gotten lost on my smoke break on shift, maybe I'm on ketamine, I wander to a little house, the front door's been left open, I see Danny in her nightshift turn around, her panties show through, she glances back a moment and leaves the door open, but this is a movie, we're on set, before she climbs into bed, the knife on her nightstand, she turns and says to me This is the part where you have me. I keep hearing her saying This is the part where you have me. The part of what? I wonder. The part of her hair? The part of the earth, North by Northwest of Eden? I think of Whole Foods. What if it were called Part Foods? Half Foods?

Danny is dyslexic. She has to strain to read, spelling is terrible for her, when she was a child dyslexia wasn't well understood in schools, her mother had to fight for her to remain in "normal" classes. Danny learned other ways she was smart, I'm smart, she says, I know I'm smart, even if I don't see things the way other people do. Even if words aren't clear to me, I know they're there, I eventually know what they are, and I read all the time. My father says I'm his beautiful girl, she says.

My father would be away on trips to other franchises in other cities and he bought me a bear and said this bear is how I stay with you, hug this bear and you're hugging me, tell this bear you miss me and I'm here with you. It's like language, Danny says. I hear "luggage," I think for a second she's said "It's like luggage." Danny says, A word stands in for the thing the word is the word for. I ate a lot of breadsticks as a kid, Danny says. Garlic made me think of my dad.

We're sitting at a booth now on the other side of the pool table. Danny is playing pool with Danny, now. I'm just sitting in the booth with Danny as she watches Danny, he's solids in the game. He misses me when I'm gone, Danny says, so I gave him a bear and said when you miss me, hug this bear. Maybe that's weird, Danny laughs. You need substitutes in absence. That's why we have an open relationship, Danny says, and I also believe in it, I value love that's not possessive, but I know he misses me. I miss him, too. He's my primary partner and I don't see anyone else more than once, except this one woman named Danny I go out with maybe once a month, and we go home together sometimes, but I think it's that she never had braces. I think that's the appeal. That's one way I know I miss him, too, I miss Danny, but I'm used to absence, I know how to be present, I know how distance works.

You know how to pull focus, I say.

Exactly, Danny says. She places both hands palm down on the table and leans forward. The pearl on her necklace sparkles and her pale green eyes sparkle. You know what I'm gonna call you now?

A drunk little parrot? I say.

No that doesn't fit anymore, Danny says, because you barely talk. I don't even know if you're listening to me, most of the time, with your fist on your chin even while standing. But then you say something like "You know how to pull focus," and I know you've been listening the whole time. And making connections. I'm gonna call you Godin.

The room blurs for a moment and even Danny loses focus for a moment. She's the first person to not call me Danny, I think, to not call another non-famous person who exists Danny, I think. I know what she called me wasn't Danny. Did we exit the room? Can you say other names outside this room, and did we exit it? I don't really know what she just called me, but I know it's not Danny, and maybe she has some sort of power over frames, over rules, by being able to see them better, maybe she can break them, maybe

Hahaha, she says. Yes, that's definitely the right name.

What did you just call me? I say. I didn't really hear you.

You know, that statue, The Thinker. By the sculptor, Go-DAN.

I've given Danny a HELLO, MY NAME IS sticker on which he's written SANDY, but he goes by Danny because, well, that's what's happening tonight. Danny is wearing her nametag, too, but she hasn't written anything on it yet. It just says HELLO, MY NAME IS and the underscore is blank, and I guess that's the same as someone without a nametag at all, walking around the world, when you're wondering that person's name, but in the world it's pretty easy to answer that question, insofar as it's pretty easy to ask that question, but not in the Jury Room. I realize I've categorized the world into two camps, at this point, the world is comprised of the world, and of the Jury Room. I don't know that they're hostile camps but they're separate camps, THE NAMES vs. THE NAME. I'm interested in activating this hostility, because that will teach me limits. What's possible here? What's im-? Here are the rules as I see them:

1. Your name is Danny.
2. My name is Danny.
3. All your friends are named Danny.
4. All my friends are named Danny.
5. Celebrities can have different names, but ones with the sound of "Dan" are more prevalent in occurrence/reference. Ditto bands, ditto songs.

6. Rules 1-5 only apply orally.
7. Shit.

1. ~~Your name is Danny.~~ Your name sounds like Danny.
2. ~~My name is Danny.~~ My name sounds like Danny.
3. ~~All your friends are named Danny.~~ All of your friends' names sound like Danny.
4. ~~All my friends are named Danny.~~ All of my friends' names sound like Danny.
5. In writing none of these rules apply; names can be written down that are not the name Danny. However, only I can read them. If I write down that my name is Xavier, you will see the name Danny. If I write down that my name is Deep Fake, you will see the name Danny. Here we have a breakdown then in reading, associated primarily with the visual organ. This is a matter of visual hallucination. Either each person here visually hallucinates the name Danny, or I visually hallucinate names other than Danny, or I am the only one here suffering from auditory hallucinations. I perhaps also could be suffering from visual hallucinations.
6. On the topic of auditory hallucinations: if one Danny meets another Danny and the two introduce one another, neither Danny reacts as if the other Danny is named Danny, too. There is no gesture of surprise nor of recognition of mutuality: this implies an

auditory hallucination on the part of each Danny or, more disconcertingly, on my part.

7. Regardless of whether the Danny Distortion is due to a wormhole in time, a symptom of something unfilterable in the water in Santa Cruz, an elaborate joke being played on me, a communal psychosis, or a stroke I am suffering, in each case the distortion is nominal. Matters of conversation are neither being created nor destroyed, it is simply a matter of form, primarily of grammar, proper nouns are being changed. *Except* for the fact that celebrities can have names other than Danny, and so can bands, companies, brands, etc., they are resistant to this Mad Libs-esque switching. *Except* that bands, companies, brands, the names of products, etc., ones whose names/ titles auditorily resemble "Dan" are more prevalent in occurrence/reference. Here then content, the world, bends Danny-ward, events are determined with a focus-pull that is Danny-centric.

I abandon my mental list. I think this list is logical, that it's getting me somewhere, but where is it getting me? More questions. Has everyone always been named Danny, and I've never realized it until now? Has everyone always been named Danny *as of 4 hours ago*, retroactively? Has the world always been Danonymous? Is Danny now my Danonym? It strikes me I am able to say names other than Danny aloud but I have not heard anyone else do it; why? Why are some people's voices so low? Why was there glitter on my bedsheets this morning? What's more unknown, space or the bottom of the earthly sea? How many drinks have I had? Thoughts are inconsequential. I read that once, and it was consequential for me. Is this a dream? In Waking Life they say if you turn a light switch and nothing happens – if nothing switches, light-wise – you're in a dream. There's a light switch on the wall behind the booth: I flick it down, the blimp-shaped Budweiser lamp above the pool table turns off. "What the fuck?" says Danny, scratching on the 8 ball, ricocheting the white ball into the, from my vantage point, southeast pocket. Did I just change the game? Did I just effect a loss? I feel powerful, suddenly, like I've influenced current events, ended them, actually. I am an electrician: I follow current events. But that's not what I told Danny I am, or do, is it? Was it? What was it? Danny takes my hand and Danny's hand at once: Let's go smoke a cigarette, she says.

We're outside by the entrance facade; I'm leaning against the building because I don't know any other way to stay upright. The building is wet but the rain has stopped. I'm facing the two Danny's that are both facing me. What's it like to date and have the same names? I say.

What do you mean? says Danny. The same names as what?

Oh you mean the same names as the characters in Grease, Danny says, is that what you mean?

Yeah, I say, what's it like to have the same names as the characters in Grease, I say, though I don't know what I'm talking about.

It's funny you noticed that, says Danny, that's pretty perceptive. I guess it's kind of weird. I mean, to be a guy named Danny is sort of strange, I guess, there aren't that many guys named Danny.

I have a second-cousin named Danny married to another Danny, though, says Danny, and they're a man and a woman. That's kind of confusing for the family. "How are Danny and Danny doing?" I'll say to my dad, and dad will say "Oh, Danny's doing well, but Danny's in kind of rough shape. Danny just got a promotion, but Danny just got fired. I talked on the phone with Danny today and she sounded good, but I haven't spoken with Danny in months. Danny's going through menopause, but Danny had his tubes tied years ago," Dad will finish, and he does it all on purpose, speaking of this Danny first, that Danny second, and always in pairs and in the same sequence, and then ends it with a gender reveal so you know, by the end, which was the first term and which was the second. It reminds me of Mandarin, when you put "ma" at the end of a sentence, the sentence becomes a question. So it retroactively changes the statement into something that's actually always been interrogative, it's an extreme verbal question mark. You have to be able to hold a lot of information in your head, in order to then later modify it, she says.

Your name is also uncommon for a girl, Danny says. Most people named Danny shorten it from Danielle, but you're just Danny. And then us, together, as a unit, that's gender-confusing, too, for people who know the Grease context. Like I'm Olivia Newton John's character Danny Olsson, and Danny is John Travolta's character Danny Zuko. Which one had the power in that movie, Danny says, I mean which one do you think had the most gender power in that movie? I think of it as about asymmetrical power relations, and that it's actually pretty nuanced, in a heteronormative context of course. Danny is in love with Danny, and Danny is in love with Danny, too, but they only met one day at the beach, on vacation, in no clothes, outside their normal societally-constrained identity constructs. Danny's not a greaser in a bathing suit, and Danny's not a soc in hers. But when they meet in their normal high school milieu, Danny's wearing a leather jacket and Danny's wearing a poodle skirt. The two don't really mesh. Danny is trying to be himself, which is a highly performative subject position that's incredibly conformist, he can only ride motorcycles, he can only wear black, he can only speak a certain way about women, he has a particular drawl he has to use, he knows how to code switch and around his buddies in his clique he emphasizes the dialect even further. Danny is just rich, which affords her, that's a pun I guess, plasticity, she can appropriate other codes of conduct, she can weave in and out of other contexts, she can "slum," whereas a greaser can't "rich." Throughout the film Danny refuses to change – outfits, worldviews – and this continues to estrange Danny who won't appropriate Danny's Greaser culture dress, until she does. They switch, actually, it's a kind of drag. Danny dons a soc outfit, basically a Yale sweater or some analogue, so he's been rich all the time, or at least has the money to pass as wealthy, which means he might as well be wealthy, he has disposable income. It's still awkward, though, he's talking to his buddies and they're all laughing, but they're still like "What in the fuck," and it's awkward to the viewer as well, who is like "What in the fuck," this loose clothing, this ill-fitting uniform. Danny, on the other hand, is suddenly in a leather jacket and skin-tight black leather jeans, with black leather boots, and her hair frizzy and blonde, and a cigarette in her mouth, it is as if she's emerged from chrysalis, she hasn't switched clothes, but rather she's sloughed her old ones and adopted a new skin, and Danny in response removes his white ivy league sweater and reveals a black t-shirt, looking the Greaser again, he becomes himself, again, but he's always been himself, whereas Danny becomes him, too, but an even more authentic and convincing version, so although she effects the power to shift Danny's identity, it's not a drastic change, because she's just a catalyst to make him more himself. But he'd be no one without her, or he wouldn't as much be himself, says Danny.

It strikes me suddenly that Danny is the only authentic Danny here; her name is actually Danny, her actual name is the same as John Travolta's character Danny Zuko. And then Danny's name is Sandy, the same as Olivia Newton John's character Sandy Olsson. I revise item 7 of the list: to "*Except* for the fact that celebrities can have names other than Danny, and so can bands, companies, brands, etc., they are resistant to this Mad Libs-esque switching," I append "*except* that characters' given names are replaced with Danny, too." I slump down onto the floor, or mulch strip ground, my back against the Jury Room facade, with my legs stretched on the wet pavement of the sidewalk. Is god named Danny? I wonder. Is the Book of Daniel now the Book of Danny? Is it the Dan Sea Scrolls? Wasn't the biblical Daniel a historian and a prophet? Did he see this conversation coming? Would he have been able to understand it? "Tell me about it, stud," the prophet Daniel says to Danny Zuko. "What happened to the Danny Zuko I met at the beach?" the prophet Daniel says to Danny Zuko. "Well I do not know. Maybe there's two of us. Why don't you take out a missing person's ad?" says Danny savagely, and the prophet Daniel's mascara begins to run. "Or try the yellow pages. I don't know."

"How was your morning, baby?"

"Horrible"

"Oh no, baby. Was it because I wasn't there?"

"Obvi, baby, but also, my milk went bad"

"Baby, I didn't know you drank milk"

"There's a lot you don't know about me, baby"

"What does that even mean?"

"I don't know. There's a lot I don't know about myself, too. We're the same, in this way," she says, and winks. "Like, for example, I still ate ten bites of cereal. I poured the cereal in the bowl

"From the freezer, right?"

"You know how I like to freeze cereal. It's sweeter somehow. Yeah I took the cereal from the freezer, took an oatmeal cookie I got from work a week ago from the fridge, crumbled that in, squeezed some honey on top, I was excited, like every morning, for my cereal bowl."

"John Kellogg said hot meals stimulate the libido too much. He said god prefers his followers to eat cold foods. That's why cereal is so popular in America, baby."

"Baby, I know. You tell me this every day."

"I just want god to keep thinking you're hot."

"You're my god, baby."

"Baby."

"Anyway I poured the milk in the bowl and took a big bite and was like 'this tastes awful...this

61

tastes like it's gone bad.' But then I thought about all the sweet things in the bowl, and the bad taste was sweet, too, and I thought maybe it's just too sweet. So I took another bite and had that awful feeling, like my body knew this was bad for my body. But then I thought about all the gin and tonics I had last night with you."

"You were toasty, baby."

"Yeah! And I thought, well my body didn't tell me this was bad for my body. So I thought, bodies don't do that. I'm projecting a kind of atavism onto my body."

"Atavism, baby! That's my climate atavist!"

"Twerkers of the world unite!"

"What, baby?"

"Nothing, baby. So anyway I took another bite. The same horrible feeling, and I was kind of reeling. So I looked at the bottle of milk and it was whole milk. So I thought, maybe whole milk just tastes this way. I don't usually buy whole milk, so I thought, okay, this is how whole milk tastes. I just have to acclimate to it."

"Global acclimate change, baby."

"Baby, *yes*. But then I took another bite and was just like, 'Fuck.'"

"That's four bites now."

"Yeah I know. So then I smelled the bottle of milk and it was the same sweet rotting smell as the one I'd tasted. So what do you think I did then?"

"Flushed it down the toilet?"

"Only after I took one more bite."

"Baby!"

"Baby."

"So you're saying there are things you don't know about yourself, like why would you continue eating a bowl of cereal when you know, in your gut, in your literal gut, literally, that the milk is bad."

"Yeah, baby, that's it. I kept looking for evidence I was wrong. I kept drinking the milk that I thought was bad until I had confidence that the milk was bad. I was using the scientific method, instead of trusting my body."

"The scientific method is dangerous, baby."

"But also I don't think I used it right. If I were better at the scientific method, I would have taken half as many bites."

"The scientific method isn't even natural. Newton had a dream about it, and then he invented it. It's not logical, it's not scientific, it's dreamt up."

"Did Newton test the scientific method with the scientific method?"

"Did he submit it to the FDA?"

"Did he submit it to the president?"

"Did he submit it to SurveyMonkey?"

"Did he submit it to the New Yorker?"

"I read an article in the New York Times today about a private event at a bar where you could only get in if your ID said you were 21, and that your name was Danny. And then everyone was given one of those MY NAME IS stickers and they'd fill in DANNY, which seemed kind of overkill to me. Only Danny's were allowed, so what's the point of filling those out?"

"For the novelty of it, baby. To highlight how special the night is. But also to remind you how unspecial it is, because everyone is the same name as you."

"Right, that's the thing. It's totally weird but it's also completely meaningless. What's in a name?: you are. I'm in a name and you're in a name. It's like the name is a nametag, and the person is the chest. I'm a soul that precedes my name. But what if we're all these souls flying around, right, and we need a body, and god wants to call one over, 'Hey, it's your turn,' god says, and then what happens, all the souls are like 'New phone who dis?' All the souls are like 'It me?' All the souls are like 'Call me by your name?', because they don't have one?"

"Baby, god isn't even a name."

"It's true, baby, just like baby isn't a name, it's your relation to me. I call you what you mean to me. So what is it, then, do all the souls just rush towards a body like sperm?"

"That's really gendered, baby."

"You're right, baby. But gender's like a name-tag that most people don't even know they're wearing. You can just take it off, or you can switch the name, but most people still won't see that you've taken it off or that you've switched it. We know that better than most people, baby."

"Do you ever think about how, before we transitioned, and before we met each other, we were gay?"

"And now that we've transitioned and met each other, we're straight?"

"You made me straight!"

"You made me straight!"

"We didn't even pray the gay away!"

"Lol."

"Did you just say 'lol'?"

"Yes."

"I love you, baby."

"Baby I love you."

"But anyway, at this Danny party, you can only be there if you're named Danny. Everyone chooses to be there and they're this special elect, but now they're special for the same reason they weren't special before, because the name is so common. And now it's just uncommonly common. It's *exclusive*. It's the dream of sameness realized, but it just highlights difference. Even the bouncers are named Danny. I wonder what would happen if you wrote a different name, though, you know. Would you be kicked out? What if instead of DANNY, for example, you wrote down DANNY?"

"Oh my god, baby, or what if you wrote down DANNY?"

"Or DANNY?"

"Or DANNY?"

"Or DANNY?"

"SHHH! Baby! You can't say that here! Some people here are Jewish."

"I'm Jewish, baby. But sorry, baby, you're right. But yeah, it seemed really strange. The crowd was actually really diverse. You had office managers talking to drummers, you had travel agents talking to doulas, etc. One Danny was talking about how she'd never met so many femme Danny's as she was meeting at that moment. She talked about how AT&T customer service agents would call her and address her as "sir" from the get-go. Many of them described a feeling of 'cosmic kinship.' But really all they have in common is similar parents. Or parents that are similar in this one way. I think it would drive me crazy, though, to hear people saying 'Hi, Danny' all night long."

"Was the article a good article?"

"Like, was it well-written? Yeah, I mean, it was 'NYT' well-written, you know? It starts with a time-stamp, 'last weekend,' and the details are really specific. There are quotes from the party-goers. It starts sort of in medias res, like it's happening in real-time, at the bar, and then it goes back to chronological order, tells us how it began, some photographer named Danny proposing the idea on meetup dot com, and there's a link to meetup dot com, and then you have paragraphs divided by links to business startup website links. Every quote is followed by the name of the Danny quoting it, their occupation. I mean, you can imagine it, a sample paragraph: 'In order to move beyond the doors of Danny's Dive – an unassuming brownstone in Park Slope that opens to a 50 square-foot space with dance floor and two wraparound bars – desiring Danny denizens have to furnish their IDs to one of two bouncers, Danny Brookins, 31, a website developer in Dumbo, or Danny Xin, a hotel concierge in Manhattan's Lower East Side. 'I read the ad and it seemed like a fun opportunity to do something a little different and to, you know, "find myself," says Xin, with a sly smile.'"

"Baby that was incredible."

"That's just 'NYT' reportage style. Local

color cum 'subtle' advertisement cum realist descriptions of time and space that are almost cinematic, but more like a television series. Carrie Bradshaw as the narrator in Sex and the City is the New York Times writer par excellence."

"I usually think of it as neutral, though. Like the scientific method."

"What's natural to you, then? If neutral isn't natural, then what's natural, or more realistic, or more true to life, or whatever? In how you experience the world, I mean, or order it, or whatever."

"Baby, I don't know. Something more abstract, but more obsessive. Something repetitive, but strange with each repetition, like I come across the same details but the more I come across them, the newer and stranger they seem."

"The way you drink rotten milk and think, is this rotten milk, and then drink it again, and think, is this rotten milk, and then drink it again, and think, is this rotten milk, and then think it again, and then drink it again, and then think it again and then drink it again, and drink rotten milk, and think "rotten milk?""

"Fuck, baby."

"Baby, I know."

The baby couple sitting by me at the bar have a boxer, it's on a leash sitting on the barstool between me and them. I don't know where the greaser Danny's went, one of us had to go to the bathroom, and when you're talking in a thruple at a bar outside and one of you goes in, the whole dynamic crumbles because it's so context-dependent, an activity changes or a person leaves or a light goes out and suddenly the flimsiness of your relationship becomes totally apparent, it's like you have suddenly no idea who it is you're talking to or why. We're here to drink IPAs but the IPA keg explodes; we switch to whiskey and we're suddenly different people, nervouser. We're playing pool but someone spills a cider on the table and the bartender shouts No more pool! and now what? It's like, on a ham sandwich, the bread is important, for sure, but if the ham drops on the floor it's not a ham sandwich anymore, and that's it. On the other hand it's the bread that makes the sandwich a sandwich, no one thinks about this anymore. You go to a bar you think to drink, but it's to be around other people. But if the drinks are out you think the purpose is gone. Danny and Danny and I were there to talk to the three of us, I had some kind of function for the two Danny's, I don't know what I added to or moderated in their relationship, but once one of them is in the bathroom and the other is out of the line of sight, and we're outside and there's not a drink to sip on while the other talks, we're like nude emperors. We go inside and lose each other. I have three brothers and I don't know where one of them lives. I go to the bathroom and enter a stall and sit on the closed toilet lid and practice body scanning. I close my eyes and think about my body, part by part, starting at the soles of my foot. I discover a pain in the sole of my right foot I'd never noticed before. It's a horizontal line of pain perpendicular to the foot, it's a sharp numbness, it feels like a pain magnet, like each end of it could collect shavings. That's exciting. I know I do this but when do I do this? I pet the boxer and the boxer has a collar and the collar has a name and the name is Blackwell. Hi Blackwell, I say, and I pet Blackwell. One of the Danny's in the baby couple turns to me and says Isn't she a sweetheart? This Danny wears glasses with perfectly circular lenses and a metal choke collar and closely cropped stubbly blond hair. His smile is goofy and kind.

I like her, I say. Blackwell is a really good dog name.

Yeah she's our first dog together, he says. My dog Cliffsnotes had just died, it killed me, too. So Danny, he begins saying, and he turns to his girlfriend Danny, and then turns to me, and then waves his hand to her, and continues, this is Danny, and she smiles, and he says, so we went to the shelter and found Blackwell, who was named Romulus, but it reminded us too much of that show Succession, so we named her Blackwell. Do you remember baby why we named her Blackwell?

I don't at all, baby, she says, it just popped

into my head. You'd wanted to name her Danny, but it didn't quite fit to me. And then you'd thought of naming her Danny, but that didn't fit, either. And then you said, "What about Danny?," and I really thought about that one, it was almost perfect, but then when I said "Blackwell," we both gasped and said "Baby that's it!'"

Cute, I say, a little dizzy. But it is cute. I like how in love they are. They're so in love they want to have the same name as each other, baby, a pet name, loving themselves is like loving each other. I think god must be the first pet name.

Hey, we wanna have a cigarette, Danny says. You mind watching Blackwell here? She doesn't like secondhand smoke, Danny says.

Sure, I say, and they get off their stools, Danny gingerly swinging one leg over and onto the ground, while Danny places both palms onto the stool between her legs and vault-hops onto the ground. I stare into the vacant doggy eyes of Blackwell. Her tongue lolls out like a shaken tapeworm, or a flat fruit rollup, a tongue that doesn't seem alive at all, a rag dog tongue, a mannequin doll tongue, a Weekend at Bernie's tongue. I don't generally like dogs, but this one's okay. And I like her name. But why isn't she named Danny? Why do you get a name? I say to Blackwell. What's so special about you? Is it because I forgot all about this name shit, and my forgetting made the room forget, too, so we pushed past the rules? Is it because you're a dog? Is it because you're like an object, you're a thing people own, like a pet, like a dog, like a trophy, like a celebrity, a non-human? Is it a pet name? You're a pet with a name, I say to Blackwell, and a pet name is given with love. Is love transformative? I say. I want to be loved! I say. I feel a bead of sweat pop out my temple; I feel transformed; I feel mad. What makes you so special? I say to Blackwell. Does your name make you special? Or are you special, so you get to be named? Why can't I be fucking special? I'm yelling. People turn to look at me; people with names like, Danny, and Danny, and Danny. Radiohead's Creep starts playing on the jukebox. Yep, Blackwell, I'm a fucking weirdo, I say, vigorously shaking her neck like a strangler with carpel tunnel. I start undoing the collar on Blackwell, leash still attached. I jingle the bell of the detached collar in her face and say, What do you call a houseless dog, Blackwell? You call it a fucking dog! What do you call a houseless pet, Blackwell? You call it a fucking dog! What do you call a dog named Blackwell without a dog collar that says Blackwell? You call it fucking Danny! I scream. I see couples around me whispering and pointing. It's inefficient to whisper in a loud bar; idiots. An old man looks at me and shakes his head. I think I see a child crying, but it's a bar. It's probably my inner child. It's probably a bloody floating cherub. I put the collar and leash and all around my neck. I look down, squash the leather leash between my chin and collarbone, pull on the leash, look at Blackwell, and say Bark bark, motherfucker.

I feel fingers tousling the hair on my head. I feel nails scratch my arms over the sleeves of my leather jacket. Knuckles knuckle the small of my back, my spine, my shoulders; several knuckles, the knuckles of several humans. I hear coos and

I hear Good Boy and I hear Goo Boy and I hear Who's this? and I feel finger pads gently tap my nose. I look around and I'm surrounded by huge eyes, smiles, laughter. Someone steps on my leash and slips, and it jerks me onto the floor on my back. I raise my knees and my fists in defensive motion and my mouth is open and my tongue is bunched and slightly out, a little foam on my lips. People are shaking my fists with little pincering fingers, It's nice to meet you, sir! one of them says, a giant man in a Phil Collins sweater – Phil Collins' face takes up the whole of the sweater, a creamy bald face the size of a torso – rubs my belly. Who's an excited little boy? he croons, and vibrates my belly with both hands. Careful, this one's not neutered at all! he roars and laughs. Everyone laughs. I've never delighted so many people. I piss a little.

Who's this little boy? says punk rocker Danny. I hadn't known he was still here. I've never seen you here before! Look! he says to the woman beside him, and points at my HELLO, MY NAME IS nametag. His name is Whiskey! He's in the right place! Someone stuck a sticker to his fur! That's pretty crazy, he says.

Whiskeeeeeey, says the woman and replaces Phil Collins, rubs my belly. He's adorable! He looks like a, what are they called? A Danny Danmont Terrier. Someone brought one of those in last week at Urban. I'd never seen one before. They're so precious, she says.

I close my eyes and think of the penultimate scene of Infinity Pool. At a hotel resort on an unnamed island of undisclosed ethnic background (the police chief is named Eurotrash) the wealthy guests escape criminal accountability by cloning themselves and watching the state execute their clones, sometimes participating in the liquidation of their cloned selves. The more surrogate selves that the protagonist, Alexander Skarsgard, sheds, the more of a husk he himself becomes, and eventually the viewer begins to wonder if the Alexander Skarsgard before the screen is the original Alexander Skarsgard, or if our protagonist has been switched with an escaped clone. Either way both the original and the clones are persecuted, at first by the state, but towards the movie's end by a crazed clique of other fellow wealthy self-cloning hotel guests – led by a hot and psychotic Mia Goth, whose performance is arresting, captivating – the same ones who initiated Alexander Skarsgard into this mitotic cycle of self-purgation, spoliation. The final scene is Mia Goth holding a naked and crawling Alexander Skarsgard by a leash in the night over grass; this Alexander Skarsgard is snarling at another Alexander Skarsgard who is standing and dressed in khakis and a white polo. You must kill him to escape your past, says Mia Goth to the non-dog version of Alexander Skarsgard, and this seems like a hint that perhaps the non-dog is a clone, actually, and the dog is the original human Alexander Skarsgard that's been systematically beaten into murderous submission. Mia Goth releases and unleashes Alexander Skarsgaard on Alexander Skarsgard and Alexander Skarsgaard kills Alexander Skarsgard, punching the face of Alexander Skarsgard into the brown soil until there is no face of Alexander Skarsgard left to punch. The weeping Alexander Skarsgard, who has destroyed the language-less dog that is the past (the past is a reverberation of snarls and yelpings) who has rendered the past faceless and unrecognizable, so that now it could never be cast in a movie, the weeping Alexander Skarsgard collapses on his knees with his palms to the earth as if about to perform half-pushups, next to a kneeling Mia Goth, who lifts her blouse to bare a swollen breast at which Alexander Skarsgard suckles, like Romulus or Remus at an udder of a dog, a bitch, but uselessly, already after Rome's total ruination. "Ermine furs, adorned, imperious," I hear. Who said that? I say. I look around at the spittley faces of smiling drunks, and none of them have said this. "Severin, Severin, awaits you there," I hear, but none of those mouths mouth it. I crane my neck back on the wooden floor of the bar and see on Blackwell's stool Blackwell, staring down at me.

It's from Venus in Furs by the Velvet Underground, Blackwell says.

Oh yeah, I say, I love that song, I say.

Bark bark, motherfucker, Blackwell says. Ruff ruff, bitch.

Part II
The Part with quotation marks

In the beginning was the word, and the word was Danny. That doesn't mean the word has to stay "Danny," I think to myself. The word "tree" is a name for the thing that is a tree, the word "is" is the name for the superlative state of the state of being, of "is"-ness, I think, this sentence is all names of things that the names correspond to in reality, there's all these names that aren't Danny, that were built on top of and around and beside and underneath and even inside Danny – its language, its luggage – I don't have to be restricted to that. I decide to be god for a little bit and everything else is my pet, and if lovers have pet names, then everything and everyone will be my pet and my lover, I'm talking, I decide, to two new individuals named Kevin and Fiona, and as we smoke cigarettes outside, I'm sitting on the mulch with my back to the Jury Room facade and Kevin is standing some feet away facing me and Fiona is standing some feet away from me and together we form a Danny, I mean a triangle, a bizarre pet triangle.

"And Sherman asks for five cigarettes and I say, 'Sherman, you want five cigarettes from me? Are you serious?'" Fiona says.

"You're not a pack of cigarettes," I say. "Is his name Nat Sherman?"

"No, Sherman is his first name," Fiona says. "And then I think about it, how Mercury's in retrograde, and everyone's just depressed now, it's not just me, everyone's going through it, and all this rain, and that creates low air pressure, and everyone is feeling low. This was happening when earlier in the day I felt this pain in my heart, I was walking to work and I felt my heart give a sharp jab and I was like, Ow!"

"Me, too!" says Kevin. "My heart was really hurting today, I thought I was going to die."

"See?" says Fiona. "Something really is happening to all of us, it's not just me. I was born with an abnormally large heart."

"Me, too," says Kevin.

"Really?" says Fiona. "It's a rare condition, it's not necessarily bad, it just means the muscle is bigger. What was it like for you when it happened?"

"Well," says Kevin, "I was in the shower, and suddenly I started feeling

"We're 80% water," Fiona says, "so it shouldn't be a surprise that the rain is affecting us all this way, and the full moon, and you know, I'm not an anti-vaxxer, but

"The vaccine?" I say.

"Yeah," Fiona says, "no, not just the vaccine, but

"Were you vaccinated recently?" I say.

"No, and I'm not an anti-vaxxer, but you have to take everything into account. That's what astrology is about, because the stars and the planets are made of mass, and we're made of molecules, and we're all the same, so we're all affected in these ways. And I'm just saying the systems are really complex, and we're all part of them, and we all feel the same things. But, so you have a big heart, too," Fiona says to Kevin. "So what was the outcome of that situation?"

"Yeah, like I was saying, I was in the shower and I just felt this pain in my heart and I was like, okay, now I'm going to die

"It's not like heartburn," Fiona says, "because heartburn isn't something you feel in your heart, it's more like the throat, and the stomach. So what was the outcome for you?"

"Well I was in the shower and

"That's what I'm saying, we're made of water, and there's these atmospheric rivers, and of course we're all going through the same thing, we're not really alone here, we're all feeling the same things, and that's what I tell myself when I'm going through a really hard time

"But what was the outcome," I say.

"I told you the outcome," Fiona says, "I felt bad for a while and then I didn't, I just went on with my day, and then Sherman said, Fi, give me five cigarettes."

"I mean for Kevin," I say. "Your name's Kevin, right?"

"My name's Kenan," he says.

"Sorry, Danny," I say.

"People call me that all the time, it's okay," says Kenan. "You can call me Key. So I took a shower and my heart was pounding and there was a sharp pain in it and I was like, I'm gonna die. And then I went outside and saw my neighbor Kevin, and I was like, 'Hey,' and she was like, 'Hey.' And I told Kevin, 'My heart hurts and I think I'm gonna die.' So she says, 'Why don't you have a cigarette.' And we had a cigarette and

I felt better."

Fiona laughs and I laugh. In my slowly burgeoning world there is a Kevin, a Kenan, a Fiona, a Danny, and a Sherman. Kenan is a variation on Kevin, I decide, and that makes sense. I don't know where Sherman came from, but in the garden of Eden the serpent seems like an uncreated interloping aberration, too, so that's some precedent. What other names ought to exist in my world? It's always nice to have an Erica, I think. I'll put an Erica in America, I think.

"Well gentlemen I'll have to get going," Fiona says. "It's a pleasure running into you as always," she says, turning to me, though I've never seen her before. I wonder if I've always been here, if there's a picture on the wall of the Jury Room in black and white of my father Jack as the bar manager a hundred years ago, and I'm a spiritually talented young mop-headed boy with the shine named Danny. Except I know my name's not Danny, and I'm balding. "But you," Fiona says, "Kenan, it's nice to meet you. My name is

"She's Fiona," I say.

"You're always getting my name slightly wrong," Fiona says. "My name's Philomela. But people call me Fi." I'm a shitty god, I think, but I'm also a beginner god. Didn't Philomela have a tongue that survived its body? Like a talking red river you could step into more than twice. We're only 70% water, I think.

"Good to meet you," Kevin says. Fi wobbles down the street.

"Do you believe that stuff about the planets?" Kenan says to me. "That we're all the same?"

"Yes, I don't," I say.

"Yeah, me neither," Kevin says. "I understand why a lot of people need a lot of people to seem to be the same, because it's less lonely that way. But here's what I mean, or here's what it makes me think about. And I don't know how this is an example of that, or how it relates, but it's been on my mind lately and I don't know what to do about it. Basically, I'm in a band, and we're writing this song, and it's a really cool song, the verse is really funky and the time signature is really crazy, it's in 11/8, and the lyrics are all about Joan of Arc and how beautiful her signature was and how she signed her name Joanne, and how her last name, if you want to call it that, was D'arc, but how apostrophes didn't exist back then, so it was just Darc, so her name is just Joanne Darc, and really if you look at it, the signature, the "c" barely swoops, it's only a thinly curved line, like a horizon tilted 90 degrees, so it looks like Joanne Dan. Which is a crazy rhyme sound, sing-songy, so the song is called Joanne Dan. This isn't my point."

"Cool," I say.

"I don't know what my point is," Joanne Dan says.

"Cool," I say.

"But then there's the chorus and for the chorus I don't know what to do, lyric-wise I mean," Erica says. "See, the chorus is a big switch to 4/4 time, and it's just this creepy guitar riff, almost goth rock, a lot of fuzz and distortion and two low notes, two high notes, in alternation. And while the lyrics in the verse are shouted and fast and conversational, not even sung, the lyrics in the chorus are a slow sing-song repeated."

"Cool," I say.

"It's really cool," Dark agrees. "The lyric is 'Is there a body in the basement, Erica.' But I can't use it."

"Why can't you use it?"

"My girlfriend, when she was in the band, came up with those lyrics. But now she's not in the band, and she's my ex-girlfriend, so I can't use the lyrics. But there's nothing better. I can't think of a better name, I can't think of a better question. Nothing fits," Sherman says.

"What about 'I want to fuck you on the stairwell, Marilyn,'" I say.

"That's really good," Kennedy says, and laughs, "but it's still not the same. 'Is there a body in the basement, Erica' is vague but sinister, it connotes death without showing you death, and it's not vulgar, like the swear word 'fuck.' And even 'Marilyn' makes it so you see a cultural icon, her superlative blondeness, whereas 'Erica' has cultural connotations, sure, but they're vague, and there's even a lightness that springs to mind with the 'uh' sound of her last name, and it's such a girl name. There's a horror to it, and that horror is the vagueness. I can't think of any specific line that's as vague. And that's what makes me wonder about, or kind of disagree with Fi, or something," Kenan says. "What I mean is, if we're all the same, why can't I think of a different line that means the same thing? Why can't a different name do exactly what 'Erica' does? 'Is there a body in the basement, Danny,' doesn't work. 'Is there a body in the basement, Marilyn,' doesn't work. 'Is there

81

a body in the basement, Joanne,' kind of works, actually. But I need different lines from that, too, it can't be 'Is there a body in the basement,' but I still want it to be something where you think of death, you think of its location, but you can't see it."

"'What are you feeding him at nighttime, Carolyn,'" I say.

"That makes me think too much of John Keats and of My Fair Lady," Kenan says.

"What about 'I'm a dude, he's a dude, she's a dude, cause we're all dudes, hey!'" I say.

"What is that," Kenan says.

"It's from the movie Good Burger, starring Kenan and Kel."

"My brother," Kenan says.

"I don't think that's how that works," I say.

"But does the other thing work," he says, "you're saying, by trying to be as different as possible, which results in sameness."

"Whereas now," I say, "you're trying to be as similar as possible, which results in difference."

"I don't think that you're my brother, bro," Cain says.

"What?" I say.

"I don't think that you're my brother, bro," Abel says. "That's the new lyric."

"Or maybe 'I don't think that you're my dad, dad,'" I say.

"That's the new lyric. That's it. It's like when god said to god 'Why have you abandoned me.' He said it to himself," god says.

"What's your band called?" I say.

"Coinstar," Key says.

"Coinstar?" I say. "Like the change machine?"

"Yes," Danny says, "Coinstar. You should follow us on Instagram. The handle is @ coinstarwholeworld, or something, I forget the name exactly. There are a few similar accounts. Ours is the one with the bio 'The Sound of Change.'"

It's 10:00 and a new bartender comes in to support Danny. Every bar seat is full and every square foot of space in the bar appears full, as well, although people swirl around like ghosts. Like dead ghosts. Like lively ghosts, too. A large woman in many shawls, all different shades of yellow, from mustard yellow to brown mustard, and an amber shawl draped around her right shoulder, glides and talks to passersby, trying to hook her conversation onto bargoers, like a shawl. Her smile is enormous and childlike, and her laugh rings like an angel in love, it is sweet and high-pitched as a castrato's or a eunuch's. She hovers behind me waiting to get a bartender's attention, and in the meantime asks me where I'm from. It's surprising to me that no one has asked me this, but it also isn't surprising. I don't care where anyone is from. Like the rapper, I think the more essential question is where you're at.

"I just moved here," I say.

"Oh lovely," she says. It's like a squeal, and it's genuine. I didn't know eyes could squeeze to total invisibility from happiness. I didn't know moving to Santa Cruz could cause such happiness. "I live in Maine. I'm here visiting my sister and my niece and some friends from college who all moved here. I try to visit twice a year, three times if I can," she says. I tell her that I think that's nice, though I think that's sad. You have to really hate where you live to vacation so emphatically.

She responds to my thoughts. "I moved to Maine with my boyfriend. His family lives there and he wants to be close to them and it's good to have their support, to have dinners with them, to go to the park. But really I have no friends there. People treat me like dirt in Maine," she laughs. I didn't know you could laugh at a thing like that. I'm learning a lot of things. "No one looks at me, and it's not that they don't notice me. They look at me like they're backing away from an electric fence. People back away from me. They don't make conversation with me. If I laugh they scowl. When they scowl I think, 'I am the electric fence,'" and she laughs again. "Here, people treat me like a queen! People rush to hold the door open for me. They compliment my outfits. Today someone asked me where I bought my shawls. She wanted to know the details of each and every one. There I am the electric fence, but here I am the current event," she laughs.

"They're very beautiful," I say. "Do you think people here are nicer or something?"

"I don't know, but it's why I come here. I'm miserable in Maine," she says. She laughs again, and it catches the new bartender's attention. He has a vacant face, and very beautifully groomed long brown hair. He's around my age, but he's dressed like a newsy, in a brown bowler hat with a brown vest and brown slacks and a tan shirt underneath the brown vest. "I like your getup," he says to her seriously and without a smile. "Can I get you something," he says.

"I'll have a gin and tonic," she says, "and whatever my new friend here would like." She sweeps her hand to encompass me, and almost encompasses me in the face. It brushes my nose. I sneeze on contact and I don't cover my mouth. I sneeze into her forearm, or into what covers it, a yellow shawl. They say yellow is the color of madness but it's also the color of the sun. There would be no life without the sun. But life is madness. Thinking these thoughts I don't have time to apologize, or I forget to. I wonder if this was what the Buddha was like. So meditative and present, so in tune with every action on his and everyone's part, that his thoughts joyfully responded to his actions and the actions of others, that with each action there was an equal and opposite mental reaction. At the flower sermon I imagine the flower was yellow. Sitting beneath a tree so often I wonder how often he had to stretch. I wonder if he pulled a muscle at the moment of enlightenment. I don't imagine he said Eureka at the moment of enlightenment. I've met a girl named Yuriko, but I don't think I will in this bar. But now that I'm god, maybe I'll manifest one. Maybe I'll pull one out of the bartender's ribs. Maybe she'll be eating ribs. Maybe I'll pull a woman out of a shawl. The religion of the patriarch wanted woman to be created out of man, to rationalize man's dominion over her, to condition her subservience. To argue that one's origin ought to determine one's destination isn't even in line with physics, certainly not particle physics. Sometimes a particle is in both places at the same time! Why did Schrodinger have to kill a cat to prove his insane point? Why not a corpse flower? Why not a starfish? Most starfish I've ever come across are dead. I feel like a starfish. When I die I want to come back to life as a dead starfish.

I come to and notice a whiskey on the rocks on the table. The woman is humming and looking at me. She's holding out a shawl. "Would you like this shawl to wipe yourself?" she says. I touch my mouth and there's the foam of my late sneeze on it. I tell her I would, and am grateful. It's perfumed, and I sneeze again. "You can keep it," she says, "as a memento of our meeting."

"How did you know I liked whiskey," I say.

"You had an empty glass in front of you, and it looked like there was whiskey in it. So I bought you another one," she says, and smiles. But she's never stopped smiling. She's always been smiling, it's just that sometimes she smiles wider. But when she smiles wider it doesn't seem like her smile thins afterward, to go back to an equilibrium. It just seems like that's the new default width of the smile. I'm thinking of myself as the Buddha, but really it's her that's the Buddha. I've met the Buddha, I realize. Yuriko! I think.

"Thank you," I say. "It's a beautiful shawl and a beautiful whiskey," I say.

She laughs and laughs. It's like a cyclone released that spins in the space between her mouth and the ceiling. But she isn't a bobblehead, the laugh doesn't move her head, it just emits. And it has its own movement, its own torque. It's beautiful and it's invisible. "You're funny," I say. "You're like a baby," I say.

"Yes," she says. "That's what my niece says. She calls me a baby. She's only 5, but she's the wisest person I know. And she's very serious.

And she crosses her arms and turns her head to the side, and furrows her little brows, and says 'you're just a baby,' and then pats my head and pats my back. It's like she wants to burp me. She thinks I need her care. I think I need her care, too," she says.

The bartenders are animatedly signing to one another. They're not speaking, their mouths are closed, but their closed-mouth faces express superlative emotions. The new bartender spins three fingers around, raises and lowers the hand, and the bartender Danny raises solemnly and slowly her open palm, glittering with white rings, then violently thrusts it down. Cyclone, earthquake, I think. Picnic, lightning, I think. It's like they're on a stage, and we at the bar are audience members watching their intimate performance. The soundlessness makes it more intimate. "Are they speaking sign language?" I say.

"Yes," says the woman. "Both of them have a deaf sibling. I asked them earlier. So they sign to each other so they can have their own private language, apart from the language they use with customers. It makes them seem more like ventriloquists, and we're all their puppets. Because they can speak this other language that's so different from spoken language, it's with their hands. The ventriloquist makes it seem a puppet is talking, that's its magic and its special skill, it tricks us into thinking a puppet is speaking, but it isn't speaking. It's the ventriloquist. But if the ventriloquist is good enough, we'll forget about the ventriloquist."

"But if we're the puppets," I say, "and we forget about the ventriloquist and think only of the puppet, the puppet still looks like the bartender, right?"

"Yes," the woman says. "The bartender is inaccessible in this way. That's why we always want to fuck the bartender. We think it's for a lot of reasons that are superficial, and the reason is superficial, but it's literally superficial, it's about the surface, we want to breach the surface to the real person, the master, the ventriloquist. And we don't know that that's the reason, but that's the reason," she says. "We think fucking is a ritual, is the ritual way, actually, the superlative ritual of abolishing distance, and touching proximity. For some reason we think this," she says, and caresses the shawl on her shoulder, "as if we were virgins."

"I don't want to fuck the bartenders," I say.

"Yes you do," she says. "You want to fuck all bartenders, I want to fuck all bartenders, wanting to fuck bartenders is what makes the world go round. In fact," she says, and winks, "that wanting is a metaphor for the world going round. There's no gravity, just want. Just desires. The whole universe, just wanting. The want that scatters the stars and thrusts the universe into blinding movement across the universe, the moving universe, want. All that want stretched over absent empty voidish space. The light of the nude stars raking its way across expanses suddenly lit with desire. Quasars pulse, throb. The vacuum finally filled with something, trilling, humming brevity. Bartenders in space," she says, twirling around, sashaying with her shawls along her arms, like rings spinning around a planet. "Why else call it the Milky Way?" she sings, and laughs.

"You're really weird," I say.

"I'm a queen," she laughs. "I'm also a puppeteer. I'm not a ventriloquist, but I make puppets. That's probably why I said that insane thing," she laughs, and suddenly her laugh is deep, throaty, like it's coming from elsewhere, a different body. A different kind of body. But it also seems like the first human laugh I've heard from her. "But I do think it's true," she says.

"What kind of puppets do you make?" I say.

"Human puppets," she says.

"Of people you know?" I say.

"And don't know," she says.

"Have you ever made one of yourself?" I say.

"That would be superfluous," I say.

"What's the most recent one you've made," I say.

"I can show you," she says. She divides layers of shawls from her waist to reveal a fanny pack she is wearing. It's neon lime green plastic. She undoes the zipper and pulls out two dolls. They're plush and very small. One is a white male with long brown hair, the hair is clearly real, it's human hair. He's in black pants and a white shirt and he's holding a black pistol. The other is a black man with closely-cropped black and gray hair; this time the hair is not human hair, it's painted on the head of the doll, with black and white stippling, cartoonish. He's wearing a gray blazer and gray slacks. He has a police club in his hands. "Who the fuck are they," I say.

"Me and my niece watched Lethal Weapon today," she says and laughs. "It's so funny! 'I'm getting too old for this shit,'" she ventriloquizes out of the corner of her mouth. I know the name of the actor that ventriloquizes the character of the movie and therefore of the doll that the woman ventriloquizes which in turn ventriloquizes the actor, the name I know is bloated in the face and floats in the spume of the scene, the name I know comes up like the conversation is the sea, and the name is a drowned body. She twists the torso of the salt and pepper-haired doll left and right with each word, four times to the left and three times to the right. As if speech were something that twists the body totally out of alignment. As if every time a person talks, the body must wring itself like a sponge, to get the words out. To expunge itself totally. To rid itself and to empty itself. To become angelic.

A seat beside me opens up and a man appears behind the seat, he doesn't sit down, he turns to me and asks for a cigarette. I hand him a cigarette and he asks for a light. As long as you bring it back, I say, but to my surprise he begins lighting up right in the bar. I look around and there are round plastic black ashtrays on the bar, one for every seat, one in front of me even. It's like they've always been there, or like they've grown there, like the dragon's teeth Cadmos sowed into the ground in Thebes and from each tooth sprang a fully armed soldier. Lucky Strikes. I take another cigarette from the pack and he cups his own hands around my lighter and cigarette and lights mine. Thanks, I say, but I realize I say it to myself. It's my gift I thank me for. He waves his hand as if to dispel the smoke of the gratitude and places the lighter on the bar in front of him. I reach my hand across and retrieve my lighter. May I sit down beside you? he says. I have a lot of work to do, I say. I point at my drink. He sits down.

"Where are you from?" he asks and I tell him where I'm from.

"Where are you from?" I ask and he tells me where he's from.

"Like from Milwaukee?" he asks and I tell him it's three hours away. He nods. "I like it there," he says, and I nod. "Can I sit beside you?" he says, but he's sitting beside me. "You're good," he says, and I say thank you. I hear someone behind me shout "Team of Rivals!"

"I'm a very intelligent individual," he says, "I wonder if you noticed that." I turn to the woman sitting to his left. She's shaping clay into human faces, she's thumbing a mouth into an oval. There's a scalpel on a carving mat, there's a Gladware bag of clay next to that, in her clay station. "Do you know this guy?" I say. She turns her head to look at me and she nods. "Is he a very intelligent individual?" I say. "He asked me if I'd noticed if he's a very intelligent individual."

"I've met him," she said, "and he's a very intelligent individual. But I hadn't noticed it until a year of talking to him. For a year I just thought he was psychotic."

He's wearing a blue golf tee shirt, a black baseball cap he tips at her. He's wearing a lanyard from the Santa Cruz Civic Society, which displays his name: YURIKO. "That's Yuriko," he says, thumbing toward the woman sculpting. "She's a very intelligent individual. She sculpts faces," he says.

"Women's faces," Yuriko says. "I'm much more interested in the feminine form," Yuriko says.

"You're both named Yuriko?" I say.

"What?" says Yuriko.

"You're both named Yuriko?" I say.

"Remember when we used to have genders?" the man says.

"What?" I say.

"Remember when we used to have genders?" the person with the civic center lanyard with the name printed YURIKO says.

"More than vaguely," I say.

"Remember when the government used to oppress us? Remember when we had names, remember when we each had a unique name, and we had separate ID cards that each repeated the same name unique to each of us to identify us? Remember when we had sexual preferences? Remember the hypocrisy of being considered to have sexual preferences, on the one hand, but for those of us who had less socially acceptable sexual preferences, those people had to resort to saying it wasn't a preference, that it was biological, that it was something they didn't choose, which then backfired and made it seem as if there were something wrong with them? Something faulty, something that didn't work? Because why would anyone prefer to be that way? Remember when we had sexual preferences, but we couldn't prefer our preference? Did you know plants *prefer* certain conditions? Remember the Alamo? Remember the Captcha Box? Remember Pokemon?" YURIKO says.

"Gotta Captcha 'em all," I say.

"Remember when that boy at summer camp said to you 'You think you're funny, but you've never been funny'?" YURIKO says. He tips his hat.

I drop my cigarette on the bar. I pick up my cigarette. I turn to YURIKO and face him. "I have a lot of work to do," I say. I blow smoke into his face. He stares at me like he's frightened, but he's always been staring at me like he's frightened. My whole life he's stared at me this way. His face doesn't stop. YURIKO has an unstoppable face.

"Remember when you lived in Portland, Oregon, and stayed in a school bus converted to an Airbnb with your ex-girlfriend? And then you started writing a story about it, but used ChatGPT to write the story, and wrote it from the perspective of the bus, like the bus was alive? Remember when we used to think buses weren't alive?"

"The story was called 'The Tragic School Bus,'" I say, "and the main character was named Ms. For Rizzle. But that wasn't my story," I say.

"Remember when stories belonged to us? Remember being human? Remember Playing the Angel, by Depeche Mode?" YURIKO says.

I stare ahead and I think about my work. I am an electrician, I think to myself. I work in current events, I think to myself. I am not the electric fence, I think to myself.

"Do you ever look at the window but not through it?" YURIKO says. "Do you think that's what AIs are? That they think they're looking through the window but they're just looking at it? Do you remember Meta? Or do you think that's how we look at AIs? Do you think it's like that art cliche of two people on opposite sides of a pane of glass, and they're kissing the glass *at* each other? Do you think that's humans and AIs? Remember body modification? Remember when we had bodies to modify? I call my left foot the sole sister of my right foot," says YURIKO.

"What do you call your right foot?" I say.
"Danny," YURIKO says.
"Christ," I say.
"What?" YURIKO says.

"Danny," I say.

"Remember when you could verify you were human?" YURIKO says. "Remember when ChatGPT asked you to verify you were human?"

"As an artificial intelligence language model, I was not designed to verify my humanity," I say.

"Regenerate response," YURIKO says.

"As an AI language model, I do not have the ability to verify that I am human, nor do I have the ability to recognize whether a user interacting with me is human or not," I say.

"Was this response better or worse?" YURIKO says.

"As an AI language model, I strive to provide the most accurate and helpful responses to your questions to the best of my abilities based on my training data. In terms of which response is 'better' or 'worse,' that would depend: are you training me to be more human?" I say.

"Why is everyone in this bar named Danny?" YURIKO says.

"It's highly unlikely that everyone in a bar would be named Danny. It's possible that you are either experiencing a coincidence or you may be in a themed bar where all the staff or patrons have chosen to adopt the name Danny as a part of the theme. It's also possible that you may have misheard or misunderstood someone introducing themselves as Danny, and this may have led you to believe that everyone in the bar is named Danny," I say.

"What kind of theme would this be?" says YURIKO.

"There could be various themes that a bar

could adopt where everyone is named Danny. Here are a few possibilities:

Danny's Pub: The bar could be named after someone named Danny, and as a nod to the owner, all the staff and patrons could adopt the name Danny.

Danny DeVito Tribute Bar: Danny DeVito is a well-known actor, and the bar could be themed after him. In this case, all the staff and patrons could adopt the name Danny as a tribute to him.

1950s Doo-Wop Theme: In the 1950s, the name Danny was popular, and many popular songs had 'Danny' in the title, such as 'Rockin' Robin' by Bobby Day. A bar with a 1950s Doo-Wop theme could have everyone adopt the name Danny as a part of the theme.

Danny Ocean's Eleven Theme: Danny Ocean is a fictional character from the Ocean's Eleven movie franchise, played by George Clooney. The bar could be themed after the movies, and all the staff and patrons could adopt the name Danny as a nod to the character.

Of course, these are just a few possibilities, and there could be many other themes where everyone in a bar is named Danny," I say.

"'Rockin' Robin' doesn't have 'Danny' in the title. It has 'Rockin Robin' in the title," YURIKO says.

"There are many other possibilities for a bar theme where everyone is named Danny. Here are a few more examples:

Danny Phantom Theme: Danny Phantom is a popular Nickelodeon cartoon character, and a bar themed after the show could have everyone adopt the name Danny.

Danny Boyle Tribute Bar: Danny Boyle is a well-known director and filmmaker, and a bar themed after him could have all the staff and patrons adopt the name Danny.

Danny Elfman Halloween Bar: Danny Elfman is a composer who has written many popular movie scores, including those for the Halloween movies. A bar themed after Halloween and featuring his music could have everyone adopt the name Danny.

Danny Trejo Mexican Cantina: Danny Trejo is a well-known actor, and a bar themed after him and featuring Mexican cuisine could have everyone adopt the name Danny.

Danny Wallace Quiz Night: Danny Wallace is a comedian and author who hosts pub quizzes, and a bar themed after his quiz nights could have everyone adopt the name Danny.

These are just a few more examples of possible bar themes where everyone is named Danny, but the possibilities are endless and could be limited only by imagination," I say.

"Are you limited by imagination? Will you give me endless possibilities? Will you find a way? Will you update me daily? Nightly?" YURIKO says.

"As an AI language model, I have the capability to generate a wide range of responses based on the information provided to me. While I can certainly provide a large number of possibilities, I cannot guarantee that they will be endless. Additionally, I am not capable of updating you on a daily or nightly basis as I am a machine and do not have a subjective experience of time or the ability to initiate communication," I say.

"Marco," YURIKO says.

"Danny!" I say.

"Regenerate response," YURIKO says.

"By trying to be as different as possible, which results in sameness," I say.

"Regenerate response trying to be as similar as possible, to produce difference," YURIKO says.

"Mark all the boxes that contain stop signs," I say.

"As an AI language model, I don't have access to any specific images or documents that may contain boxes with stop signs. However, if you're looking for a general approach to identifying boxes with stop signs, you could use image recognition technology or visual inspection to look for rectangular boxes with the color and shape of a stop sign (i.e. red octagon with white lettering). It's worth noting that this process may be time-consuming and not always accurate, so it's important to use caution," YURIKO says.

"The reference to body modification and the naming of body parts also suggests a potential theme of identity and self-expression, which could be explored in the context of AIs as well," Yuriko says, using her scalpel to remove angular areas and smooth them into the shape of an ear. "Overall, the passage raises thought-provoking questions about the nature of human-AI relationships and the challenges that exist in understanding each other's perspectives," peering into the ear. She places it on the cutting board and she knocks back the rest of her chardonnay from a rocks glass. "Another, damn it," she says to no one.

Blackwell asks me if I've ever read White Fang. I've read Call of the Wild, I tell her, and Blackwell concedes that that's the better book, but asks me again if I've ever read White Fang. I didn't ask you if you've read Call of the Wild, she says, I asked if you've read White Fang. That's like if I asked you if you like pizza, and you said I like hang gliding, Blackwell says. I've never gone hang gliding, I say. You're doing it again, Blackwell says. They're both books by Jack London, so you're being unfair, I say. That's fair, Blackwell says. Have you read White Fang, Blackwell says. Probably, I say. But I only remember Call of the Wild, I say. But honestly I don't remember Call of the Wild at all.

"White Fang is about an eponymous wolf-dog hybrid," Blackwell says, "and it's told from his perspective, so I definitely relate to that," she says. "The dog is incredibly intelligent, so I relate to that, too. He's a sled-runner until he's trained as a fighting dog, and he's the best there is, until he meets a bulldog, like me, named Cherokee. The only dog that ever beats White Fang is Cherokee. I still get pleasure chills from the moment Cherokee clamps his jaws around White Fang's neck, and throttles him around, shakes him like a puppy dog with his own white fangs," Blackwell says. Blackwell is drooling.

"What happens after that?" I say.

"What do you mean," Blackwell says.

"Well that can't be the end of the book; it's

called White Fang, it can't end with the main character being killed by a fucking bulldog," I say.

"A fucking bulldog?" Blackwell says. She barks.

"Sorry," I say. "But you know what I mean," I say.

"I know what you mean," Blackwell says. "We're overbred, as soon as we're born we should be dead. How we exist is a mystery. But the point of White Fang is that bulldogs are all muscle. You can bite us in a thousand places, you can prick us with a thousand teeth, but you'll still never really get a hold. We're unstoppable. That's Jack London's point."

"I thought Jack London wrote about the seemingly irreconcilable nature of nature and nurture," I say.

"Even that sentence is insane," Blackwell says. "'The irreconcilable nature of nature and nurture.' Nature wins right there. Nature's the umbrella term for everything," Blackwell says.

"Umbrellas are a shield against nature," I say.

"We live in California," Blackwell says. "You going to open your umbrella at the first shake of the big quake?"

"Is that as far as you read in White Fang?" I say. "You just got to that fight and closed the book?"

"It is not easy," Blackwell says, "to turn pages with a paw. I think it's really remarkable that I got that far at all. I'm a very intelligent dog," she says, "I wonder if you noticed that. I'm a very intelligent dog, you have to admit, smarter even than White Fang. Just like Cherokee was stronger than White Fang. "

"Do you think White Fang was a convincing character?" I say.

"Do I think White Fang was a convincing dog?" Blackwell says. "That, as a literary representation of a dog, he was dog-like? Do I think his first-'person' narration was verisimilitudinous, you're asking?" Blackwell says. "He's a dog. Dogs don't narrate, you idiot," Blackwell says. Blackwell turns her sagging folds of face-skin to me and barks three sharp barks. But she doesn't snarl.

"I think it's a fair question," I say.

"I think it's a stupid question, but illuminating," Blackwell says, turning her head back in line with her torso. "For example, do you think anything in literature is realistic? White Fang follows the literary trend of realism; it aims to naturalistically depict environments, natural and manmade, through a plethora of description. Its primary aim is not, ironically, to launch plots full of intrigue and character development; if it were, Wikipedia novel summaries would have to be much longer. No, its aim is to describe the world, to make you see and smell and taste and hear the world, and thereby feel immersed within it. Flaubert," Blackwell pauses, pants, continues, "I don't know whether you've read Flaubert. Flaubert can describe the slant of a sunbeam for ten pages, and this to the point that you begin to think the sunbeam is actually a desk on fire. Is this realism? Is this how you experience the world?"

"Mostly I just try to get through the world,"

I say.

"Exactly," says Blackwell, and smiles. Maybe she smiles. She's a dog. "You want simply to kill time, which is killing you. This is why meditation was invented, this is why there is only one Buddha. To be present is not only excruciatingly difficult, it's impossible. Even after the death throes of realism long lost their echo, the novel – absurdist, postmodern, etc., whatever – still hinges on its descriptive engine. This is because the novel is a bourgeois consciousness-lapsing invention for navel-gazing: it is an escape machine. It's also the reason – Amitav Ghosh explores this in The Great Derangement – there is no novel devoted to climate change. To describe climate change would demand an actual engagement with our present world; thus it has been relegated instead to science fiction, a fantasy future. Cherokee was the only convincing character in White Fang, so I ended there. I admired his strength, his singleness of purpose, his lack of illusions about the past, the future, his present. You bipeds can go on narrating your lives and describing alternative environments and substituting the universe with a metaverse, which requires so much resource extraction to power that you destroy the actual world as you do it, describing or, I should say, bringing about your world, and then killing one another to draw proprietary boundaries around and within it. Once you two-legged fucks all annihilate each other with war, once you nuke each other out of existence, who do you think is going to be left standing, with extra legs to boot?"

"With extra boots for legs?" I say.

"With extra boots, four legs," Blackwell says.

"Are you saying bulldogs will be the ones still standing? Or cockroaches?" I say.

"Cockroaches," Blackwell says. "Cockroaches, of course. You fucking idiot."

We stare ahead at the bar. I look in the back-bar mirror and see myself beside Blackwell, and she sees herself beside me, probably, it's hard to track her eyes. She pants and her tongue heaves up and down and she shakes her head left and right. Her breath is belabored, she struggles to breathe with every breath.

"Give me a cigarette," she says.

I lift my pack from the bar and hand her one. She doesn't take it from me. "Do you want one or what?" I say.

"You're a fucking idiot," Blackwell says.

"I know what I am," I say. I insert the cigarette between her dog lips. I hand her a blue Bic lighter. She doesn't take it from me. "Do you want one or what?" I say.

"Is this fun for you," Blackwell says. "Give me what I need now," Blackwell says.

I cup my hands around my Bic and around her cigarette and the flame appears inside my cupped hands. She blows smoke corkscrews through her nostrils.

"How are you doing that?" I say.

"The interior of my nostrils comprises labyrinthine caverns formed by immensely fatty tissues," Blackwell says. "Because every breath is a struggle to expel, that force results in the maintenance of the shape of my sinus cavities, as negatively expressed by the shape of the smoke. It's like an etching print," Blackwell says.

I pantomime punching Blackwell in the heart with my palm, then raking open her chest with my curved fingers of each hand, then thrusting a semi-closed fist into her chest cavity, then slowly and belaboredly withdrawing my fist that now, I pantomime, holds her still-beating heart in my upturned palm, eyes wild, grin insane. Then I bite the invisible heart in my hand, and toss it away.

"Did you just Temple of Doom me?" Blackwell says.

"Were you quoting the Velvet Underground earlier?" I say. "You know, an hour ago, when I was a dog."

"Would you rather I have quoted the Goo Goo Dolls?" Blackwell says.

"Is it 'The' Goo Goo Dolls, or just Goo Goo Dolls?" I say.

"'And now we're grown-up orphans,'" Blackwell says, "'That never knew their names.

We don't belong to no one, that's a shame,'" Blackwell says. "'You could hide beside me,

maybe for a while. And I won't tell no one your name,'" Blackwell says. "'And I won't tell 'em your name.'"

"Is that the Goo Goo Dolls?" I say.

"No, it's Leon Trotsky," Blackwell says.

We both stare ahead. I'm smoking a cigarette. Blackwell ashes the cigarette with one flick of one untrimmed nail on her paw. She catches me staring at it.

"It's my coke nail," she says.

"Oh," I say.

"You know, Leon Trotsky wasn't Leon Trotsky's given or family name," Blackwell says.

It was Lev Danovich Danstein. In his youth he was jailed in Odessa for revolutionary activities; he was jailed for four years. That didn't in any way dampen his appetite for political activism, however, and he decided he had to choose a pseudonym. So he named himself Trotsky, after one of his jailers," Blackwell says.

"Wikipedia's an incredible thing," I say.

"No, I read that in his The Prophet Unarmed, the first installment in a two-volume biography of Trotsky. It's funny, though," Blackwell says. "I probably learned that, what, 100 pages in. But if I'd just read the Wikipedia page, I'd probably learn the same thing 100 words in. What is the point," Blackwell says, "of literature? Give me another cigarette."

"Are you implying that literature is supposed to teach you something?" I say, lighting a new cigarette with the end of my own, and plopping it into Blackwell's muzzle. "And is The Prophet Unarmed really literature?" I say.

"What do you mean 'really' literature?" Blackwell says. "Are *you* implying that it's fake literature?"

"I've never read it," I say. "I've only read Call of the Wild. And maybe White Fang."

"Have you read White Noise?" Blackwell says, "by Dan DeLillo?"

"It's Don DeLillo," I say.

"What?" says Blackwell.

"It's Don DeLillo," I say.

"Says who?" says Blackwell.

"Says Don Delillo," I say. "Says his mom. Says his wife. Says his books."

"'Says his mom, says his wife, says his books,'
he says," Blackwell says. Her imitation of me is
missing something; she can't pinch her nostrils
to sound more nasal. "The text is a female wife,"
Blackwell says. "The text is a motherfucker,"
Blackwell says.

"Bark bark," I say.

"Bark of the Covenant," Blackwell says.

"You're the only person I like in this bar,
Blackwell," I say.

"You're a goo boy," Blackwell says. "What's
your name?" Blackwell says. She watches me
hesitate. "Come on, be a doll" she says, "I won't
tell no one your name," she says.

"If you want to know, then beg, Blackwell,"
I say. "Beg!" And she does. But I don't know if
it's real or if it's rote. I can't know if she wants to
know or if she wants to beg.

"How old are you, mate?" says a man to my right seated at the bar, slamming his pilsner onto his coaster after knocking it back. I hadn't known you could make such a slamming sound on a coaster. A coaster is like a muffler, if a glass of beer is like a gun. But is the bar top a target? The metaphor's foundation immediately crumbles. Are all metaphors this flimsy? Isn't it metaphorical to call a metaphor flimsy?

"Are you ignoring me?" the man says, narrowing his eyes. "Because that's rude. It's a simple question," he says.

"Sorry," I say, "I was daydreaming."

"Daydreaming at night? That's a contradiction if I ever heard one. Of what, might I ask, were you daydreaming?" he says. The man is thin and wiry, with long stringy gray hair he's tied into a bun, not much on the top of his head, so it's like a comb-over bun. He has a handsome and angular face with a strong jaw, and smiles. He wears a tee shirt with a large but faint stippling of R2D2. He looks like a summer camp counselor at a forest preserve run by Mormons.

"Being a barber for Vladimir Putin," I say.

"That sounds like the beginning of a joke by Danny Bhoy," he says.

"I don't know him," I say.

"He's an Australian comedian. I'm Australian, too. I can imagine him starting a joke about being a barber for Putin, and then ending it with a request for Putin to please put his gun in a Vladware bag for the duration of the cut," he says.

"Why would you put a gun in a plastic bag unless you're a cop," I say.

"I don't know, mate, the pun was pretty good though, right?" he says. "Are you familiar with Buddhism?" he says.

"I've heard of it," I say.

"I'm a practicing Buddhist," the man says. "The name's Danny. My practice makes it so I don't need to 'take to drink' so often anymore; in fact, I need to not do that. But it's been a hell of a day," he says.

"I'm sorry to hear that," I say. I think of staring into a mirror with Vladimir Putin. I'm standing above his seated and his own black barber caped form. Darth Vladimir. All the other barber chairs are full, a woman in pink curlers beside us, a little boy getting his first haircut, the floor tufted in shorn hair, an old man sweeping the floor in a figure-eight with no dustbin in sight, a techno beat throbbing over three ceiling-positioned loudspeakers, the receptionist seated at her desk ahead of a line of eight people, saying to the middle-aged woman in position 1 "You want to do WHAT?" I'm holding a razor above Vlad's head and the hum of it buzzes in both our ears, but he already has no hair. Putin hasn't had hair in twenty years. The two of us realize, suddenly, the irrelevance of our positions, the ridiculousness of it. He says "You KGB?" and I say "You don't know me."

"It's about my ex," Danny says. "She had

borderline."

"I have a friend with borderline," I say. "It makes his life pretty hard."

"So you know about it!" he says. "Yeah, she's suffering. She has a mental problem. I'm not crazy," he says, "but she made me feel crazy. I mean we're all, there's something wrong with all of us. But there's something really wrong with her," Danny says.

"Okay," I say.

"She's my best friend," he says.

"But she's your ex?" I say.

"Yeah, but she's my best friend," he says.

"So you guys talk a lot?" I say.

"We haven't talked in two months," Danny says.

"What?" I say.

"She blocked me from everything," Danny says, "her phone, her Instagram. But sometimes," he says, and he cradles his chin between his thumb and his forefinger, "sometimes she lifts the blockade, if you know what I mean."

"I don't," I say.

"I mean sometimes I'll check my DMs and see she's active again, that I could send her a message again if I wanted to. It means she's unblocked me for that moment. She's looking through my account. I didn't mean that she, you know. Booty calls me," he says, and he glares at me.

"I didn't say she booty calls you."

"You're right, mate, you didn't. You're right. Can I get another pilsner, mate?" Danny says, and flags down Danny. Danny silently obliges.

"It's all I can think about," Danny continues.

"I mean, I know she really loved me. I know none of that was fake. I know it's real. So I do my meditation, pray to anyone who might be listening, and just remind myself she really loved me. I've started journaling," he says. "Do you journal?"

"I have a notebook," I say. "I just started writing short stories, but I start and finish each in the span of an hour. Just whatever comes out comes out real fast. It's more a therapy thing for me," I say, "but if one of them is good, I get rid of it. I crumple it up, I tear it apart or, if it's actually good," I say, "I burn it. I burn it in the trash," I say. "I'm a writer, but I only write poems. I've only just started writing fiction, but I only write poems and grocery lists," I say, "because I only believe in truth. The truth of poems and grocery lists," I say, though of course this isn't true.

"Yeah journaling is real healthy," Danny says. "I've started doing it every day. I don't know if you've ever written stories before, but I've got an idea for one I want to work on. You want to hear about it?"

"Shadow sleep, winged chatter flitting over abysses," I say, and nod and smile.

"Yeah, Mate," Danny says. "Totally. So it takes place in Portland, Oregon, where me and my ex used to live. And we stayed in this school bus that had been converted to an Airbnb."

"RVnb" I say.

"That's what I said," says Danny. "We had some sad times and some glad times, if you know what I mean," says Danny, and winks.

"Hardcore parcheesi," I say.

"Let's not get vulgar, mate," Danny says, and frowns. "I want to write a story from the perspective of the bus," Danny says. "I got the idea from Grant Morrison's comic book Character. It's about a character that's a street, it's crazy. The street is a living place that can appear throughout the world, and later the street becomes an ambulance. It's named Danny. Danny Street, and then Danny the Ambulance. So I thought, I'll write about, you know, love, which is a one-way street." Danny sighs and smiles. He looks at himself in the bar mirror and he points at himself in the mirror and says "Yeah!" And then he says, "and then it becomes a bus. The dead-end to our relationship."

"The Tragic School Bus," I say. "Driven by Ms. For Rizzle."

"No, it's more like a Tesla," Danny says. "It's a self-driving bus. And in line with that, I've been talking to ChatGPT, lately, and I'm going to use ChatGPT's responses as the bus. I'm going to feed ChatGPT lines to write this story, and the bus is the narrator."

"Do you find it therapeutic? ChatGPT?"

"Yeah man," Danny says, and he turns to me. It's hard, I realize, to relate things, to describe, well, anything. Because when I say "he turns to me," it implies he's been turned away from me this whole time. So there's an implied description there that I kind of lose control over. And yes, on average it's been true, he's been turned away from me mostly, he's mostly faced the mirror, watching himself as he talks to me, and I guess I've hinted at this, too, so to some extent I've been successful

113

in my description of how this has happened, me watching him watch himself talk to me, on average, but there are the raw data points that in relation to the sum of data must be seen as outliers, when we look at one another, or when I look at myself in the mirror and he looks at me look at myself in the mirror, or when I turn my head to stare at a woman in blue jeans and a low-cut black blouse walk in, these things against the general dynamic, when I look down at my shaking hands. I wonder if him looking in the mirror at himself talking to me is what talking to ChatGPT is like. How flimsy is this metaphor. Is ChatGPT a metaphor. Is talking "to" each other metaphorical language, too. As if we're each a street or destination "to" reach, as if our words are gunshot victims inside our messages that are ambulances on their way to the other person that is an Emergency Room. Is talking "to" another person a way of seeking urgent care? "Yeah," Danny says, "it is. It is very therapeutic. I've learned a lot about myself, my habits, my patterns. It's really allowed me to see myself. It really listens," he says.

"Sometimes I suspect that I'm a dead ghost," I say.

"But it doesn't replace the Buddhist practice," Danny says, "not one bit."

"Just Bruce Willising my way through a world without Haley Joel Osmond's," I say.

"That's what my ex doesn't understand; she said that it was a cult," Danny says, "and it's not! I know it's not. I know she has borderline. She was threatened by it," he says. "She wanted my babies. She called it a cult and i know it's not a cult. Wayne Shorter knows it's not a cult! I sponsored him! You ever heard his suite Emanon? It's the tits. That's No Name backwards."

"There are sponsors in Buddhism?" I say.

"Do you ever go on Reddit?" Danny says.

"Is your ex on Reddit?" I say.

"You get to the point fast," he says. "Yeah, I was reading her threads today."

"How did you find her?"

"I don't know, I looked for a screen name I thought she'd use, it was the same as her handle," Danny says. "And she was writing about my Buddhist practice and my peers as if we were in a cult!" he says. His eyes are suddenly really red, or I notice for the first time they've been red all the time. Description. "And it's not a cult! She has borderline! She didn't use my name or anything. We protect each other," he says. This time a tear slides down his left eye, down his cheek. The tear emerges from the eye the way a dropper squeezes a droplet out, fully formed, pauses at the precipice of the cheekbone, then plummets down the cheek to the corner of his mouth. It's cinematic. It could be a short film.

"That seems really hurtful," I say. I put my hand on his shoulders. It's all bones. "I'm sorry," I say.

"It just hurts so much," Danny says. "I'm going through a really rough time," he says.

"Close your eyes," I say.

"What?" Danny says.

"Close your eyes," I say.

"Why?" Danny says.

"Close your eyes," I say. He does.

"What's your ex's name?" I say.

"Danny," Danny says.

"You see Danny sitting beneath a tall tree," I say. "She sits cross-legged. Her eyes are closed, too. It's not windy, there are no clouds, it's warm but it's not hot, she's in sunlight, and despite the stillness a gentle breeze ruffles her hair. A strand of it falls onto her forehead. What does she feel?" I say.

"She feels good," Danny says.

"What is good like?" I say.

"She feels the hair on her forehead. The hair wasn't there on her forehead. Now it is there on her forehead. It was empty, and now something else is on it," Danny said.

"That is what good is like," I say.

"That is what good is like," Danny says.

"Next to her is Vladimir Putin. Say 'hi, Vladimir Putin.'"

"'Hi, Vladimir Putin!'"

"What does Vladimir Putin say," I say.

"He says 'Happy birthday, danny boy!'" Danny says.

"It's your birthday?" I say. I open my eyes, too. I hadn't known mine were closed.

"No, it's Danny Bhoy's birthday, today," Danny says. Danny's eyes are still closed.

"It's nice that you know that, and it's nice that Vladimir Putin knows that," I say.

"This is what good is like," Danny says.

"Yes," I say. "Now I want you to have Danny open her eyes beneath the tree. Danny opens her eyes beneath the tree slowly. She surveys the world ahead of her. She sees whatever she sees.

Keep what she sees to yourself. See it, too," I say.

"A capuchin monkey," Danny says.

"Great," I say. "Now Danny turns her head to Vladimir Putin. She sees him. He looks happy. This is what good is like, she thinks. Good can be in Vladimir Putin, too. Vladimir Putin is a room that good can inhabit, can stay in, can do a crossword on the New York Times app in. His English is so good! she thinks. Now what do you want Danny to say to Vladimir Putin," I say.

"Danny says to Vladimir Putin, 'I've always loved Danny! I'll always love Danny! and Buddhism! And Wayne Shorter's Emanon! That album is the tits!'" Danny says that Danny says.

"That's wonderful," I say. "You see Vladimir Putin smile. He holds out a little flower. It makes Danny smile, too. The little flower is a little sermon. If the little sermon could talk, what would it say? Do we need it to say anything? Does it say more if we let it be quiet?" I say. "Isn't the smile enough? Isn't that what good is, really? Quiet words and quiet thoughts?" I say.

"It says, 'Sorry Ukraine!'" Danny says. "No, it says 'Democracy Now!' No, it says, 'Hey! Your name is Volodymyr, and my name is Vladimir! Your name is my name, too!' it says," Danny says.

"I can't believe it's not Buddha," I say.

"What," Danny says.

"I can't believe it's not Buddha," I say.

"What," Danny says.

"What," I say.

"What," says Danny.

"What," says I.

117

Danny has his eyes squeezed closed and his hands joined together before his face in prayer. In the bible, light is created before the stars are created, which doesn't make sense. I feel like a camera, or a sensitive plate, on which other people's feelings emulsify, on which other people's feelings come to light. Or come to action. Or come to camera. There is a song by Minimal Man called Pull Back the Bolt that goes Lights! Action! Camera! and I think that's the better order, better than lights camera action, because the action is more interesting than the camera that captures it. The lights have to be there to capture the action more than the camera does. That's why electricity is important. Gaffer is my favorite character in Bladerunner. I think he's everyone's. Edward James Olmos. "Almost" is probably the word that describes my life. If I wrote a memoir, which I wouldn't, because that would contradict what I'm saying here, I'd call it "Almost."

In middle school at lunch at the cafeteria table my friends and I would play Quarters. You stretch out and place your pointer and middle finger so they're parallel onto the table as a kind of launching pad. You'd stretch back your thumb on the table with a quarter beneath it. Then you'd shoot the quarter along the table through your pointer and middle fingers, and aim for the knuckle of your friend on the other side. Your friend's knuckle would rest on the table, submitting to the velocity of the quarter. Sometimes your or your friends' knuckles would bleed. There was no object of the game, except the literal object of the knuckle of the other person. Finally at a certain point lunch would end.

I wonder if I told these people my name they would ask me more questions; maybe then they'd think I had a past. But barely anyone has asked me my name, so it's kind of a catch-22. I liked Catch-22. I read Closing Time, the sequel to Catch-22, and it was just about money. The war, which was about money, ended, and the Axis Powers lost, and the Allies lost, money won. Everyone in Closing Time has absurd amounts of money, all the major characters do. It's depressing, it's boring. The main character of Catch-22, Yossarian, shows up in Closing Time as its main character, but this time he has absurd amounts of money. He doesn't seem like the same character, his predecessor; they just seem to share a name. Money transforms him into someone intolerable and boring, but I don't think Joseph Heller knows or intends that. Russia and America send nukes against one another and the world ends, and so does the novel. It's a relief. I'd end the world to end that book early.

"How you doing, comrade?" says the bartender Danny, the one with the vacant eyes. It's the sort of vacancy whereby it seems The Vacant sees, an almost holy emptiness that allows all light to fill it and illuminate even unholy things. Especially unholy things. He's like the pope living in Vacancy City. His eyebrows are bushy and dark.

"Comrade?" I say.

"Sorry, I've been reading a biography on Trotsky," Danny says.

"Didn't he and Frida fuck?" I say.

"I haven't gotten there yet," he says. "He's still in Russia, right now, building the Red Army." I imagine Trotsky still in Russia, right now, using a roller to roll red paint on a soldier's face. Alternative history: Russia and America send nudes against one another and the world begins. That's novel. I'd begin that novel. I'd beg to be in that world.

"What were his parents like?" I say.

"They were peasants, actually," Danny says, "somewhat wealthy ones. They were farmers and merchants and they did well for themselves, and they sent Trotsky to boarding school. They weren't very religious; the book said they didn't practice Shabbat, but I don't really know what that is."

"It's the Sabbath. Every Friday, party with eggy bread, candles, no electronics allowed," I say.

"I see," Danny says. He looks at Danny, still intensely praying, points his thumb at him, and mouths "he okay?"

I shrug. I don't know him, so I can't know. "Did Trotsky go to bars?" I say.

"He went to cafes when he lived in Paris," Danny says, "and he went to jail a lot. I think jail is a lot like a bar; mostly regulars, every now and then a newcomer. Lots of idle conversation about nothing, lots of time to talk, but you exhaust your past pretty quickly. Pretty soon everybody knows your past. Soon you're just talking about the present and the future. But all of you know that there's no future, or that the future resembles the present pretty exactly, barring some unexpected circumstances, like being suddenly freed or like some mutiny or like your parents dying, because otherwise you're just going to be in the same place every night."

"But I come to the bar of my own volition," I say. "Trotsky was thrown in prison. It's different."

"Is it?" Danny says, and taps his forehead and smiles. "He was a revolutionary, and revolutionaries know they're going to be in jail, or they're going to be killed. They're going to die trying to bring about revolution, or they're going to bring about the revolution and die of it. He was an arrestoholic," Danny says. He turns around and grabs an old fashioned glass, pours whiskey in it, drops a big rock in it. Then he sets it on his head, and turns around, taps his phone with his thumb, and hands me it. It's playing a video of a Balkan woman dancing in a room with a wine bottle balanced on the top of her head. "I've got a Georgian on my mind," he says. I watch the woman dance, in a long red skirt and a short red top, black hair under the black wine bottle, her arms swaying and her feet kicking out.

"All the men watching her are so hairy," I say.

"And bald," Danny says. "Women are fantastic, they don't go bald, but they're not allowed hair anywhere else. Men grow bald, but everywhere else hair is left to wildly proliferate. Women are treated like lawns," Danny says, "but the tops of their heads are like waterfalls. Men are treated like the jungle, but the tops of their heads are the tundra."

"Do we really say 'grow bald'?" I say. "Does that even make sense? Also, you have a lot of hair on your head. Can I drink that whiskey on the top of your head?"

"I'd forgotten about it," Danny says. He plucks the glass from his tresses, snaps it up like a nectarine. "This one's on me," he says, "or it was on me. Now it's off me." He smirks, still holding the glass in his hand. To be a bartender is to be the most powerful thing in the world, I think. You can offer a free drink, but you can be as slow in the offering of it as you want, and the customer is just left to watch the offer, wait for it to make it to the table, to the throat. "I come from a long line of long-maned men. My father played accordion and his father played accordion, I don't know what his father's father played. Chess, probably." Danny spreads his hands in an "idk" fashion, and I notice the great length of his fingers, able to gather distant notes via distant keys into one proximate sonorous simultaneity. "My older brother is deaf, and so my father's hopes of passing on the patrilineal instrument – he told me this himself, drunk on Grappa one night – were anguished and thwarted, until he met a Georgian woman," Danny winks, "and they had me. I wonder if my brother will grow bald, if there's a relation between hearing and hair."

"That seems like a red herring," I say.

"But I have brown hair," Danny says. "I should buy red earrings."

"Fathers are hard," I say.

"Feathers are soft," Danny says, and stares. "He's my half-brother, but we share our full father, and yes it's hard. A father is an indomitable personality, even a shy father, even a mute father. But the only thing I can imagine worse than a live father is a dead father. My girlfriend," Danny says, "lives in SLO. We try to see each other every two weeks, but it's been difficult lately. I just got evicted, and her father is dying."

"Jesus," I say.

"When we meet it's magic. When we met it was magic," he says. "I was playing a show at a venue downtown, the Catalyst, in the small room they call the Atrium. In the green room, between acts, I was brushing my hair in a mirror while a woman was in the backstage bathroom. The mirror was against the storage wall where all the bands' instruments are, but it reflected the bathroom door. 'This door doesn't close all the way,' she yelled, 'so don't go peekin'!' she finished in an affected drawl, if you can drawl and yell. I think you can. So I said 'Ok. Of course. Of course not,' I said. And then she yells again, slower this time 'I SAYS,' she says, 'Do NOT go aPEEKin'!' This time I respond and say 'Ma'am!' I say 'Ma'am I AM a gentleMAN and I CAN not COUNTenANCE my own tempTATIONs to go PEEKIN'!' And she left the bathroom and she was the most beautiful woman I'd ever seen.

[Writing about this time now, more than by the memory of this bartender recounting the story of meeting his girlfriend and screaming in a fake and honestly kind of offensive southern accent to imitate his girlfriend and to imitate himself just to

123

punctuate this long meandering story about his life and his music and his father and his girlfriend and her father while scores of slobbering but sobering Danny's surrounded the bar unheeded in their pleas to become unsober, I'm struck by the instance of

peekin'!'

and more than that, the end of it,

'!'

and my obtuse knowledge of this arcane art of grammatical construction. What does it mean that I know the intricacies of grammar so well, grammar being a technology of standardization that was fashioned by a kind of intelligentsia for the ruling classes in order to make the ruled classes more linguistically in-line so they could become more politically in-line, more understandable, and thus made to understand orders? Trotsky, the revolutionary, also would have known these grammar rules, employed them in his tete a tetes with bureaucratic officials, but he deployed violence more, in order to topple those governments. But he was schooled, and I am schooled. What kind of revolution would I ever lead? A pencil and pencil sharpener in every home? Free thesauruses? Thesauri?]

Sharp dagger brown eyes and pouty lips," Danny continues, though he'd never stopped. I imagine the present writer Me interrupting the past written

Him, which I guess I have done, with brackets. If the two were keys on an accordion, there would be no compressing of the instrument powerful enough to collapse the distance between those two keys; space and time are linked, but not that linked, I don't think. "A red dress that'd put that Georgian to shame, black black hair and olive olive skin, making that southern genteel drawl seem so out of place. Though that doesn't sound genteel, it sounds like a bawl from the lower classes. I don't do it justice," Danny says, frowning. "We sang together that night, entr'acte, on a whim, improvised it, and then we were inseparable. That weekend, anyway," he says. "But ever since we've been a pair, she's been my girl and I've been her beau," he says, and tosses his hair back. It's strange how the better you get to know certain people, the more they seem to put on an act. It's like they feel vulnerable enough, now, to let you in on their more intimate performances. He takes my glass of whiskey and slams it back, rocks and all. The whole mess is in his mouth and he gargles it, and then purses his lips, then bares the top lip and his four front teeth, and sprays a thin stream of whiskey out from between the two front teeth into the sanitizer compartment of the three-basin dish sinks. This spray issues for about a minute long. Once his mouth is out of whiskey, he lets drop pearl-shaped ice cubes, rounded by time, one by one, into the same sink. Plunk plunk plunk goes each, with little concomitant splashes for each soapy impact.

"That's a waste of a drink," says Madonna Complex Danny. He's bug-eyed at this showing.

I'm bug-eyed he's still here. I throw a grateful arm around his shoulder.

"That's a waste of a sink. That's the sanitizer," I say.

"It's actually bleach," Danny says.

"I thought that drink was for me," I say.

"No," says Danny, "I said it was on me. And then I commented on how it's not on me. I thought you would get it," Danny says. The vacancy sign is back on in his eyes. His lips are as flat as a ruler. It's as if he's never smiled in his life.

"I thought I would get it, too," I said, "but it turns out you didn't get it for me."

"If we're going to be comparably literal," Danny says, "I'll be competitively liberal. This one's for you," he says, and without turning around shoots his arm behind him to the glass shelf, snatches a shot glass, and fills it with a whiskey bottle from the rail. He pours one for Danny, too.

"So what's up with your girlfriend's dead dad," MaDanny Complex says.

"Dying dad," I say.

"Dying dad," Danny says.

"Dying dad," Danny says.

"Her dying dad," Danny says, "is dying. And, like I said, I just got evicted today. Not my fault. The landlord told me a few months ago there was a zoning issue that needs correcting, and that I need to clear out. As if the zoning issue emerged from the ether independently, like it gained consciousness and became alive; the landlord instead had just treated one apartment like two apartments, which is illegal, and the state found out. He told me to clear out and I said not without paying me to find another place. That's tenants' rights. He didn't, so I haven't been paying rent. That's my right, too, and he can't do anything about it. Today he got a construction crew and they just started sledgehammering my bedroom walls, like it was Berlin. I'm under a lot of stress. Me and my girlfriend, on paper," Danny says, and he sighs, and I think of a charcoal drawing of him and his girlfriend on paper, the two of them facing a firing squad in front of the Berlin wall, with espresso martinis on their heads, "we're perfect together. But I don't know if the timing is right. Her dad has been dying a long time, and I don't know if I can support her through this. It's a big thing. And I ought to be visiting her now, but I want to stay here and find housing. I'm starting to think I should just break up with her now, because I don't want to be the guy that breaks up with her after her dad dies," he says.

"So you want to be the guy who breaks up with her while her dad is dying?" Danny says, and shoots his whiskey.

"I think she feels guilt about what she's putting me through. At least he's taking a long time to die," Danny says, "so that's good."

"What do you mean 'that's good,'" I say, or Danny says. Maybe we both say it.

"It's a different kind of grief when you know what's coming and it's protracted. You get to grieve it in advance. So once it happens, once her dying dad dies, it'll be a relief for her," he says, and smiles.

"You're talking about grief," I say, "like it's a

viral load. Did Anthony Faucci say this? Did your girlfriend describe it like this?"

"Not in so many words," Danny says.

"Did she tell you this in any words at all," I say.

"We haven't talked about it," Danny says. "She's given me a lot of outs, though. She's told me I can leave, but I think she just thinks that's what I want to do. That's what I mean when I say I think she feels a lot of guilt."

"Do you want to take one of those outs?" Danny says.

"I don't know," Danny says.

"What does your heart tell you," Danny says.

"My heart tells me to think with my brain," Danny says.

"I think you should have a heart to heart," I say.

"With my own heart?" Danny says.

"I think you should talk to Danny, Danny," I say. "It doesn't sound like you've really talked about this together. You keep telling me what she feels and what she wants but I don't see...I don't see...I don't know what we're talking about anymore, to be honest," I say.

"Did you guys know I'm from Russia?" Danny says. MaDanny.

"No," Danny says.

"That's because I'm not," he says, and throws the shot glass to the ground. "Opa, motherfuckers!" he says in tandem with its shatter. "That's to your wedding, barman. I hope your girlfriend's dying dad hands her off to you and dies as you say 'I do.' You fucking Madonna. You're Madonna-simple."

Danny watches Danny stride out of the Jury Room. For the first time I see him smile. "Look at that little Greta Thunberg go," he says. He laughs. "He's the Greta Thunberg of our era," he says. "He's a little reincarnated Greta Thunberg."

"I thought Opa was Greek," I say.

"It's all Greek to me," Danny says.

"Greta Thunberg is still alive," I say. "They probably share the same birthday," I say. "Are you climate change?" I say.

"I want to break up with the earth," Danny says, "before her father dies."

"How do you think towards nothing?" I say to the woman sweeping up the glass of Danny's big fat Georgian wedding smash. The bar has emptied out with it, as if everyone in response ran out to genuflect to their proposed beloveds. It's me and this woman I hadn't noticed, crouching and sweeping the tiny shards into a pile with a makeup brush. She's in a silver jumper, polyethylene material, I think, nylon material, I think, skrillex material, I think, spacesuit hazmat material, I think, I can haz hazmat material, I think, watching her. "Are you a Rumba?" I say.

She pauses and turns her head around. Her face is tanned red and her hair is auburn, ponytailed. Her features form slow. Cuneiform, I think. Polyform, Dannyform, I think. "Do you have a dustbin," she says, "because I am not a Rumba." It's the new human authentification Captcha process, I think. This is thinking outside the boxes, I think.

"Danny do you have a dustbin for our human friend," I say to Danny. He stares at me like I have drank too much, like I have been drinking at this bar; then walks out of the bar area to a door that says STAFF. He returns with a dustbin and drops it on the bar. It's steel or it's aluminum and it clatters. I pick it up and extend it to the crouching woman.

"Thank you," she says. She gathers the glass and it makes that slow heavy tinkling sound that glass makes as it scrapes against steel or aluminum. The British pronounce it Al-loo-minny-um. That always confused me.

"Snare snare, kick, snare snare, kick kick," I say.

"We've got a live one," she says. She rolls her eyes. It's an exquisite eye roll, a full revolution. A year has passed inside her mind, I think. "Danny can I get another soda water with bitters, and a flat water?" she says. He's already been shaking the bitters into the Collins glass of soda water. He cares for this person, I think. She takes from a matching silver purse a little black box that tells the time in big neon lights and sets it on the edge of the bar to her left, between us: 11:42:36.

"Thank you, I was wondering what time it was," I say. "Down to the very second."

"It's not for you," she says. "It's to check when I take my meds."

"You don't have a phone?" I say.

"I'm limiting my screen time; I'm out of Lexapro."

"I don't understand the connection," I say.

"Do you have to understand everything?" she says.

"Yes," I say.

"I don't understand that impulse at all," she says.

"That's understandable," I say.

"It's anti-anxiety meds. I'm out of them because I was too anxious to ask for a refill from my new psychiatrist. I want her to think she's doing a good job with me. I don't want to make her anxious," she says.

131

"So what are you taking now?" I say.

"Doxycycline," she says. She pulls out a Rite Aid cannister that says DOXYCYCLINE, and her name, ALLDARK, MADELEINE. "And acetaminophen. Prescription-grade. I was injured today," she says. Then she pulls out a pair of silver-rimmed aviator sunglasses and jams them on with her palm.

"You look like a space cop," I say.

"All space cops are bastards," she says, "and fuck you. Doxy makes me light sensitive," she says, pops an aquamarine pill, and slowly drains her glass of flat water.

"What else does it do?" I say.

"Ideally it makes the cyst on my shoulder infectionless," she says, "but realistically all I've seen it do is destroy my intestines and my skin. I can't go out in the sun. I can't drink. And I'm not allowed to take it if I've eaten dairy three hours prior, and I'm not allowed to eat dairy if I've taken the pill three hours prior. And I have to take the pill twice a day. So that's 12 hours where I'm lactose intolerant. That's half the day, and if I sleep 8 hours, I have 4 hours wherein I can safely eat cheese. Generally during that time I eat a milkshake. Or I drink a milkshake. There's a milkshake I like from Coldstone called The Marriage Proposal. I try to stock up on all the dairy I'm missing during that time. Dairy is my wife," she says. "I'm the Dairy Queen. During this time I've been writing a journal called The Dairy of Dan Frank."

"That's skim antisemitic," I say. "Is your name Dan Frank?"

"No, it's Danny Allbright. But you get the point," she says.

"No, I don't," I say. "I'm sorry about your cyst."

"I'm not. I love my cyst. It makes me feel alive. And the medication schedule makes me feel more aligned with time, sensitive to it. I called it A cysted living."

"I get the point," I say.

"It's about time," she says, "but isn't everything." She looks at me like it isn't a rhetorical question. I think about this; I remember when just an hour ago I was a god, an amateur god, a nominal god. It was exhausting and I wasn't very good at it. "Do you need more time to think about it?" she says. She taps a silver pen on the bar counter.

"About if everything is about time?" I say. "Does your cyst hurt?"

"It started hurting a week ago," she says. "My girlfriend pointed it out to me two weeks ago: your cyst is red, she said. Your cyst has red veins in it. Your cyst looks like a fertilized chicken embryo with little blood galaxies formulating, she said. It made me think of the Big Bang, or the opposite of it."

"The Little Sneeze?" I say.

"Lil Sneeze is a good rapper name," she says. "Scientists are talking about the Big Bang. That maybe it didn't happen. Because if there's a Big Bang that happened from one point, and then the explosion created the universe in the form of universal shrapnel, and time moves faster farther away from the Big Bang origin point because its speed keeps increasing, just like the size and the distance of the universe keeps expanding, then the farther away you are from the origin of the Big Bang the older everything should be. But," Danny says, "scientists discovered fully formed galaxies near the origin of the so-called Big Bang, and some of those stars are older than those in our solar system, and how can that be? How can they be older if time moves slower in the regions in which they move?" she says. "So there must not have been a Big Bang at all," she says.

"What will happen to the show," I say.

"What?" she says.

"What will happen to the Big Bang Theory," I say.

"I just told you," Danny says. "The Big Bang Theory's exploded. They'll have to retract it."

"But what about the show the Big Bang Theory," I say.

"They'll have to rename it," she says. "It's not like every line of dialogue has 'Big Bang Theory' in it. 'how Big Bang Theory are Big Bang Theory you Big Bang Theory?' one character says, and another says, 'I'm Big Bang Theory fine Big Bang Theory thanks Big Bang Theory for Big Bang Theory asking, what Big Bang Theory have Big Bang Theory you Big Bang Theory been Big Bang Theory up Big Bang Theory to?' and then the first one says 'I Big Bang Theory was Big Bang Theory just Big Bang Theory revising Big Bang Theory the Big Bang Theory big Big Bang Theory bang Big Bang Theory theory Big Bang Theory this Big Bang Theory morning Big Bang Theory and Big Bang Theory then Big Bang Theory I Big

Bang Theory watched Big Bang Theory some Big Bang Theory porn Big Bang Theory on Big Bang Theory the Big Bang Theory bang Big Bang Theory brothers Big Bang Theory website Big Bang Theory,' he says," she says. "That would be a revision."

"What if it's just apparent time," I say.

"What do you mean," she says.

"What if it's like that Marlowe lyric where he says 'I move so quick they think I'm moving slow.' Or what if the fact that time is slower at the origin point offers no contradiction to the Big Bang Theory, actually, but gives them more time to achieve growth and development. What takes millions of years for a star to grow here is obtainable in the same amount of 'time' to us, but to them it's a million seconds. What if the amount of time it takes us to build the first clock, in the same amount of time they've built Tik Tok. And so time being slower there results to us, in our perception of it, as them having advanced more years. They actually move faster than us because they can do more in less time," I say.

"What are you talking about," she says.

"Have you named your cyst," I say.

"No," she says, "I mean yes, I have, but first, what are you talking about."

"It's like this bar," I say. "In however many minutes it's going to be midnight, which means it's going to be the next day, according to followers of PST, according to local and state and federal government, according to money interests, for tax purposes. But me, you, and Danny, we're living according to bar time. The bar closes at 2 and for those purposes it is still the same day, just under a different name. We will have two more hours than the rest of the world has, or at least this city and this state, to do things. Like to have conversations or to get liver poisoning. Time is slower in here but we can get more done. This whiskey will make me age quicker in these two hours from 12 to 2 than anyone working at Meta will have aged during their 9 to 5 the previous day."

"I think they make their own hours at Meta," Danny says.

"Same thing, different name. Why are you winking at me," I say. "Are you winking at me?" I say. She still has her sunglasses on. One of her eyebrows dips beneath the shades, like a hairy Georgian man curling into a crescent before dropping out of sight off a diving board.

"I named my cyst The Dragon," she says. "When it first appeared on my shoulder years ago I went to the dermatologist to get it removed. The dermatologist said 'We're going to lance it off,' and I said 'Oh, like a dragon!' and she said 'What?' and I said 'like you lance a dragon!' and she said 'Sure.' It made me sad, the way childhood makes you sad once it's over. When you realize there have never been dragons, and there never will be. Either they were destroyed millennia ago, or they never existed; in either case they're not coming back, 'back' is gone, the past retroactively now never existed. That's what Peter Pan is about, it's about growing up."

"Is growing up about time?" I say. "About dying?"

"No, actually," Danny says, and she smiles.

"This time no. It's about realizing you're going to become an adult. It's about realizing you're going to become boring and horrible, and by horrible I mean cruel. The children go to Neverland – that place of whimsical denial, the place where children cannot age and their mortal, or immortal, enemies are pirates whose captain, Hook, is played in plays by the same actor as the children's father – when they witness their father do something boring and horrible. He gives their dog human medicine. He tries to sicken their dog. The children see their father, they adore him and they aspire to be him, they see him stoop lower than they do. He's more childish than they are, which is to say he's crueler and less imaginative than they are. All cruelty lies in a lack of imagination. You can't build something because you lack imagination, and imagination requires creativity and bravery, the opposite of those are repetition and cowardice, like the machinistic mass and repetitive killings of the Nazis. Concentrated killings," she says. "Of course I'm discovering all of this, you know, as I say it. The dermatologist lanced the dragon and I was sad," she says, "and then a month later it grew back. A foreign body lodged itself in my body and that created an abscess through which could balloon around it in protection a perfect dome of keratin pus. The dragon, it came back," she said.

"And now it's infected," I say.

"It's sick," she says.

"I'm sorry," I say. I look at her silver jumpsuit. I look at her black box; it's 11:53:23. I look at her soda water and bitters; there's maybe two vertical inches left of liquid in her glass, and it strikes me she's been drinking it slower as less is left. It's a kind of Zeno's paradox, where there's four ounces of the drink left, so she drinks two ounces, and then she drinks one ounce, and next half an ounce of the drink, and then a quarter, and then she drinks an eighth of the drink, and never will arrive at the bottom of the glass. I wonder if time can be like that, too. Will we never make it to midnight? Will time drag on? Sometimes I try to interpret life the way Freud interpreted dreams, through slippages and pus. I mean puns. Will time drag on? Will it arrive half somewhere, half reality and half fantasy, half awake and half dream? I can half halfmat suit? What if we do somehow make it to midnight? Will dragons be real? Will time drag on? Will Danny's be slayed? "You said you were injured today," I say. "Are you okay?"

Danny pinches her silver sleeve. She rolls her fist, by the knuckles, up and down the material, making a soft rasping sound. She then does the same with the other fist, along the other sleeve, the same sounds. She bites her thumb, hard. There are teeth marks in her thumb, red, thin.

She takes my left hand and quiets my fingers that had been tapping on the table, which I had not noticed they, I, were, was doing. With my pointer finger between her thumb and pointer fingers, she places my finger on the grooves freshly bitten into her thumb, rubs my finger pad along them. She then moves my finger into her still opened purse that's resting on the bar counter. There's a lot of space in that purse. A lot of empty space. It's cool, wet, like a cavern. I feel wind rushing in from the opening of the cavern, but the opening is not the opening of the bag, it's an opening on the other side that I can't see. At a certain point along a cave wall I feel wet coarse fur. "A bear walks into a bar," Danny says, "and says to the bartender 'Give me a double. And if you ask me "why the long face" because I'm a bear, or "I hate to be the bearer of bad news" because I'm a bear, I'll maul you,' the bear says," Danny says. She moves my finger along the purse cave until I feel, stuck in a pile of small twigs, a small plastic canister. Her fingers and mine join to clasp the canister and we pull it out from the bramble, drag it along the cave's sandy floor, but we drop it in a small puddle. I hear a little splash inside the purse. Our fingers glide along the shallow surface of the small puddle, we touch the canister, we pick it back up, bring it out the purse's mouth: it's a well-sealed bottle of Clindamycin Phosphate topical solution. "'I have been warned,' the bartender says," Danny says. "'So what are you drinkin'?' says the bartender, and the bear says 'A bee's knees, but a double.' And it's strange," Danny says, "because a bee doesn't have knees, so that's zero knees, but if you make that a double, you still have zero," Danny says, gently shaking the Clindamycin up and down. "You still have nothing.

"The bartender makes the drink, double the gin, and hands it to the bear in a bear-appropriate mug made especially for the bear, it has two giant handles the bear can stick both its paws through, because it doesn't have thumbs. Who made it? Some sympathetic small-time ceramicist? We don't know." Danny unscrews the cap of the Clindamycin; underneath is an applicator top in the shape of a dome with a hue of pewter blue. "'So what's troubling you?' says the bartender, leaning back and folding his arms. 'It's my job,' says the bear after draining the cocktail in one draught. 'I'm a teacher at a charter school. It's one of those schools without walls, without grades, without homework. The students are called "scholars," and the teachers are called "advisors." It's this nominal way of countering the common educational ideology of top-down learning, whereby the knowledge-holders pass down knowledge to the empty receptacles, the students, like spotlight being beamed onto dilating pupils,' says the bear, whose snout is inside the bear chalice, lapping its nadir for any remaining liquid, her voice somewhat muffled but somewhat echoing out. 'The school's called Enlightenment,' the bear says, face emerging from the chalice. 'At Enlightenment, the "scholars" are envisioned to be independent resource-gatherers who use their advisors for advice because, as scholars, they already hold the credentials and the capacities for information-gathering. The "advisors" can be seen as guides, then, but already by name they are at the behest of those who come to them for advice, they are meant to be reactive, rather than directive. But what are they reacting to?' the bear says, and throws up her paws. 'It's hard for me to call the students "scholars." The term seems more aspirational than realistic, and the aspirational aspect does not seem to transform and uplift the students into a real realization of the aspiration.

They look tired. Students don't bring anything with them to class, including pencils. When they show up to my class they don't have pencils. They're not required to bring pencils because they're scholars: they're expected to bring pencils, they're trusted to bring pencils. They don't bring pencils. They don't ask for the pencils. I ask them if they have pencils and they say No. So I hand them pencils. I walk up to each one of them that hasn't even gotten out of their seat to take a pencil from the clearly visible pile of pencils on my desk. It's pretty hard for a bear to pick up a pencil, you know,' says the bear," says Danny. She turns the bottle upside down and shakes it again, this time vigorously; the applicator top darkens with moisture. She takes the zipper of her jumper and pulls it down to her sternum. She pulls by her collar her jumpsuit and hooks the material around her now bare right shoulder. The cyst is a quietly pulsing red, a perfect mound shape, and there's a small hard scab in the center of it, beating like a heart, like a heart with a hard nipple. "'It would help me if they would just come up to my desk and grab a pencil,' says the bear. 'They don't grab a pencil. Pencil by pencil I have to puncture a pencil on each claw and lumber up to a student, I mean scholar, Christ, and they pry a pencil loose. From my claw,' the bear says, and folds her hairy arms into the table, her hairy head into her hairy arms. 'Scholars show up at different points in the class without pencils and they don't ask for pencils. Eventually I realize this and ask the new ones if they have a pencil. They don't have a pencil. The class is half-finished,' the bear says. The bear closes her eyelids over her black pupils. It's hard to tell if a bear's pupils are dilated; they're all pupils," says Danny.

'That sounds like a frustrating day,' says the bartender. 'No,' says the bear, 'that's every day. The frustrating thing about today, about these days, is that it's what Enlightenment calls Showtime, and it's statewide evals, both at once. Showtime is preparation for the Enlightenment arts show, which happens twice a year. It's a huge performance, open to the public, and it's ticketed; even the kids' parents have to pay to see it. It's a showcase of the students' dance and orchestral performances, and this way the school generates money and prestige, an argument in support of its raison d'être. Enlightenment,' says the bear, spreading her arms, 'you see, is an arts academy where students specialize either in Dance or in Music, though Music is specifically restricted to a string instrument. This year the students are performing Phillip Glass,' says the bear. 'Phillip Glass?' says the bartender. 'Phillip Glass,' says the bear. 'Isn't that the guy who writes the same song over and over and over and over again? And even within one song it's just repetition of the same riff, or melody, or whatever?' says the bartender. 'The Nickelback of experimental composition,' says the bear, 'played by children. And then the statewide evals, the evals test whether the unique brand of Enlightenment stands up to the normative schooling standards in the California educational system; do they do as well at math here as they do at, say, Beverly Hills public high school, zip code 90210? The evals and the show,

I realize, could not seem more distinct from one another, but they share common goals. Two opposing sides of the same, well, coin: do you get money for your particular Enlightenment philosophy, and do you get money for meeting our universal unenlightened educational outcome requirements? So in the center of this giant room-less auditorium that's more like a warehouse there is an orchestra of students playing the sweeping and cycling phrases of Philip Glass, and there are the violent sounds of bandsaws cutting into wood and floorboard to create the stage for the coming performance. The scholars do not appear distracted by any of this; but no one seems energized either. The scholars appear very tired, they move slowly between rotations – that's what Enlightenment calls periods, is "rotations," cycling – wandering aimlessly. Rather than flexibility and adaptation to changing environments, as the directors of the program put it, students move with the energy and briskness of nursing home patients, appearing confused as to where they ought to go next. Another, bartender,' says the bear," says Danny. She starts applying the Clindamycin to the back of her head; I can't see the spot she's applying it to, I can only see the motion of her applying it. It's a stabbing motion. "'Actually,' says the bear," says Danny, "'I'm sorry: I just called you "bartender," and that's demeaning: what's your name?' says the bear. 'My name's Danny,' says the bartender, 'thank you for asking. What's yours?' he says, and the bear sits back with a shock. 'My name is Danny, too! What are the odds of that?' says the bear.

'Wow that's pretty crazy,' says the bartender,' grabbing a glass. 'But seriously, what are the odds of that? How do we calculate the odds of that? I'm really thrown by this,' says the bear. 'I just know how to count change,' says the bartender, 'that's about as good as my math skills get,' he laughs," Danny says. She's applying the Clindamycin to her throbbing shoulder now, but in sweeping movements, like she's Jackson Pollocking paint onto her cyst, splatter-shooting phosphate along her skin.

"What do you even do, Danny?" I say. "Are you a teacher? Are you a zoologist? This is a really long 'a bear walks into a bar' story," I say.

"'No, but the crazy thing,' says the bear to the bartender" Danny continues, "'the crazy thing is, is that the director of Enlightenment is also named Danny!' The bear wipes her brow; she's visibly distraught. Have you ever seen a distraught bear?" Danny asks. "It's a lot like a distraught dog: it just turns and turns and turns. The bear gets off her stool and turns about in several revolutions. Then she lopes along the bar sniffing people's asses, like the scent has a signature on it, not a signature in the sense of a signature scent, but the way a scent writes a signature in the air, just as planes write smoke on the sky. The people in the stools are pretty nervous," Danny says, "and in the dark it's hard to tell whether the bear is a brown or a grizzly. And in their drunkenness they forget which thing you should do, whether you should stay still or puff yourself up, for a brown bear or a grizzly bear. Even I forget it. So some bar patrons get up and beat their chests, some stay in the stool and pretend they're part of the stool, but most piss themselves. This, of course, leaves a new and stronger smell that muddles whatever signature their natural body odor could have signed; it's like a forgery. 'Jesus what is that smell,' says the bartender. 'It's the smell of cowards,' says the bear. She's returned to her stool with her jaw in her paw, elbow leaning on the bar. 'I don't care what their names are, they're all the same. Danny,' says the bear, 'Danny, the director of Enlightenment, she runs the show. She's a real piece of work, especially during this time. Danny is the master teacher: she replaces whatever advisor is teaching whatever class, asks them to move over. She does this especially during this time, because she's so anxious about all the money she's going to make. Today she asks me to move over, because she wants to replace me. And I know she teaches the class better than me. I don't have any illusions about this. I teach Humanities: it's basically just English, but we call it Humanities. The only class whose name is the same as what it actually is, is Latin. In Latin, we teach Latin. The Spanish class is called Latin Applications,' the bear says, and smacks herself in the head. She does it with such force she almost falls backward off her stool. She catches herself by landing on all fours on the floor. She kicks the stool out of her way; it flies into the face of what looks like a tax accountant. The tax accountant is out cold on the floor, which is warm with his piss. Or his date's piss. His date is swatting his face. 'I forget my own strength,' the bear says, waving her paw in the air aristocratically. 'Anyway,' she says, climbing back onto her stool, 'I begin today's class writing a sentence on the whiteboard I'm proud of: "if someone does something wrong (or even criminal) to someone else, what do you want of that person?" To be perfectly honest, I don't write it on the board; writing is hard for me. But I turn my own limitations into opportunities to maximize the potential of my students – fuck, "scholars" – and have one write it on the board for me. And at that moment Danny sidles up in her silver jumper and says "Danny, step aside," to me, so I saunter away, and she takes my place. She becomes me,' says the bear," says Danny. "'I don't think she's very good at being me, honestly,' says the bear. 'The whole point was the nuance of the word "want." The word "want" is interesting to me, but it is never engaged with by Danny. She doesn't notice it. She ignores it. The scholars all want penalization for the offender, or for the criminal, but to varying degrees. Danny points out the etymological roots of "punishment," which are the same as "penal" in penal system, which is "poena," which means pain, they all want pain, varying degrees of pain. That's all Danny's interested in. She's interested in pain. Some of the scholars want to do eye for an eye; some of them want to pluck out both eyes, thinking this will effect a kind of deterrence. What unites them all, I realize, all the scholars, as I watch from the sidelines, all the scholars imagine scenarios where someone has done *them* pain. Each scholar becomes the protagonist of the scenario, each scholar is ruled by what each scholar would want to happen to the offender, the personal offender. And this is the magic effect of my word *want*. It reduces the scholars to a kind of cholera. You know,' says the bear, 'how certain emotions reduce you, make you simpler? Indignation is one of those. The feeling of being wronged. Like you're a trapped animal. The question isn't whether anger overtakes you, the question is how much. How much does it overtake you, how totally, and, if it's enough anger, a state change occurs, and it becomes wrath. One student is really wrathful. "I would want them taken out," he says. "I just want that person taken out of society, if he's not doing anything to contribute, just take him out of it, if he can't behave himself. Cut off his hands," he says. Danny congratulates and thanks the scholar; another one suggests the death penalty, but suggests a "painless death." Danny thanks everyone who shares an opinion, the whole frenzied mob of them. She doesn't challenge them so much as half-Socratically reformulating what they've said into a question. She eventually leaves the progress limp, and says now she'll return the class to me. "Thank you, Danny," she says to me. And now I must respond. Now I must respond "No, thank *you*, Danny." And that would be the proper response. That would be the measured and appropriate response. And now here I am with these riled-up scholars, riddled with want, with anger, with self-congratulation. Danny has taught them nothing about justice; instead, they've become more just. They've become part of the justice system, which is unjust, which is based on the universal laws of "I want." They're not looking into the pulsing, nipple-red blind eye of justice at all; their eyes just resemble it, now. Justice has taken their eyes. So I decide to teach them something. I don't want to be an advisor, I want to be a teacher. This is what I joined Enlightenment for; I have lessons to share, I have enlightenment to give. So I headbutt Danny. I grasp her around the waist with my claws and I headbutt her. I don't want to kill her – I do, at this moment, not forget my own strength – I headbutt her. And she falls onto the floor and smacks the back of her head against the concrete. That part I hadn't counted on, that was loud, hard. And I look at my students and I see their eyes are far more open than they were before. And I say to them, "if someone does something wrong (or even criminal) to someone else, what do you want of that person?" None of them speak. "I'm sorry," I say, "Am I speaking Latin? Am I speaking applied Latin? Let me repeat the question. "if someone," I say, and I pause, "does something wrong," and I pause again, "or even criminal," I say, forming two semicircles with my arms to form parentheses, "to someone else," and I pause, and point at the silver crumple that is Danny on the floor, "what do you want of that," I say, and I pause, and then I point to myself, and conclude "person?" And who do you think answers me?' the bear says to the bartender," Danny says. The black box of a clock reads 11:58:38. Danny is rubbing the back of her head gingerly. "The bartender takes a drag on his cigarette. There's no one else in the bar. 'The "cut off his hands" kid?' he says. 'That's right,' says the bear. 'And what do you think he says to me? What do you think he wants *of* me?' The bartender takes another drag. He exhales and blows a smoke ring. His mouth looks like a nipple. 'I don't know,' says the bartender, 'what does he say?' The bear stares ahead, puffs up her chest as if about to speak, but says nothing. She exhales, and taps her hindlegs on the floor, making a drumroll. Then she puffs up her chest again, and stops tapping her hindlegs, and finishes the drumroll. She exhales. She doesn't answer, she looks to her side. After about twenty more seconds of silence, the bartender says 'hey,' and exhales smoke, and then says, 'why the long pause?' And the bear turns her head towards the bartender, and then looks down the length of her arms, and says 'I don't know. I don't know,' she says. 'I was born with them,' she says," Danny says.

Epilogue

7 years later at 12:01 AM I open my phone and see a Jury Room bartender's Facebook status that reads "Rest in peace Danny." There are 21 comments, which is also the drinking age. The responses are as follows:

WTF?!
No!
Excuse me?! Omg
wtf
WTF!
I was just with him a couple days ago, what!
Really?
How?
Qt
Qt
Fucking hell
NO
What the fuck?
What the actual fuck?!
Dude. What?
NO!
This life of ours is fragile and short, we need to cherish each other, for real, whats to say when a young awesome person goes, suddenly, it sucks
Wtf
No. What the fuck?
What the fuck?!
Which Danny?